SUBCONSCIOUS FEATHER

An Anthology Curated by

Aishwarya Patro

Inkfeathers Publishing
www.inkfeathers.com

Subconscious Feather
Edited & Compiled by Aishwarya Patro
Print Edition

First Published in India in 2022
Inkfeathers Publishing
New Delhi 110095

www.inkfeathers.com

DISCLAIMER

The anthology 'Subconscious Feather' is a collection of 16 stories, 6 articles and 36 poems written by 38 authors who belong to different parts of the world.

The anthology editor and the publisher have ensured to make the content as reader-friendly and plagiarism-free as possible. Unless otherwise indicated, all the names, characters, objects, businesses, places, events, incidents- whether physical/non-physical, real/unreal, tangible/ intangible in whatsoever description used in this book are either the product of the author's imagination or used in a fictitious manner. Any resemblance to actual persons, objects, entities, living or dead, or actual events is purely coincidental.

The stories, articles and poems published in this book are solely owned by their respective authors and are in no way intended to hurt anyone's religious, political, spiritual, brand, personal or fanatic beliefs and/or faith, whatsoever.

In case, any sort of plagiarism is detected in the stories, articles and poems within this anthology or in case of any complaints or grievances or objections, neither the anthology editor(s) nor the publisher is to be held responsible.

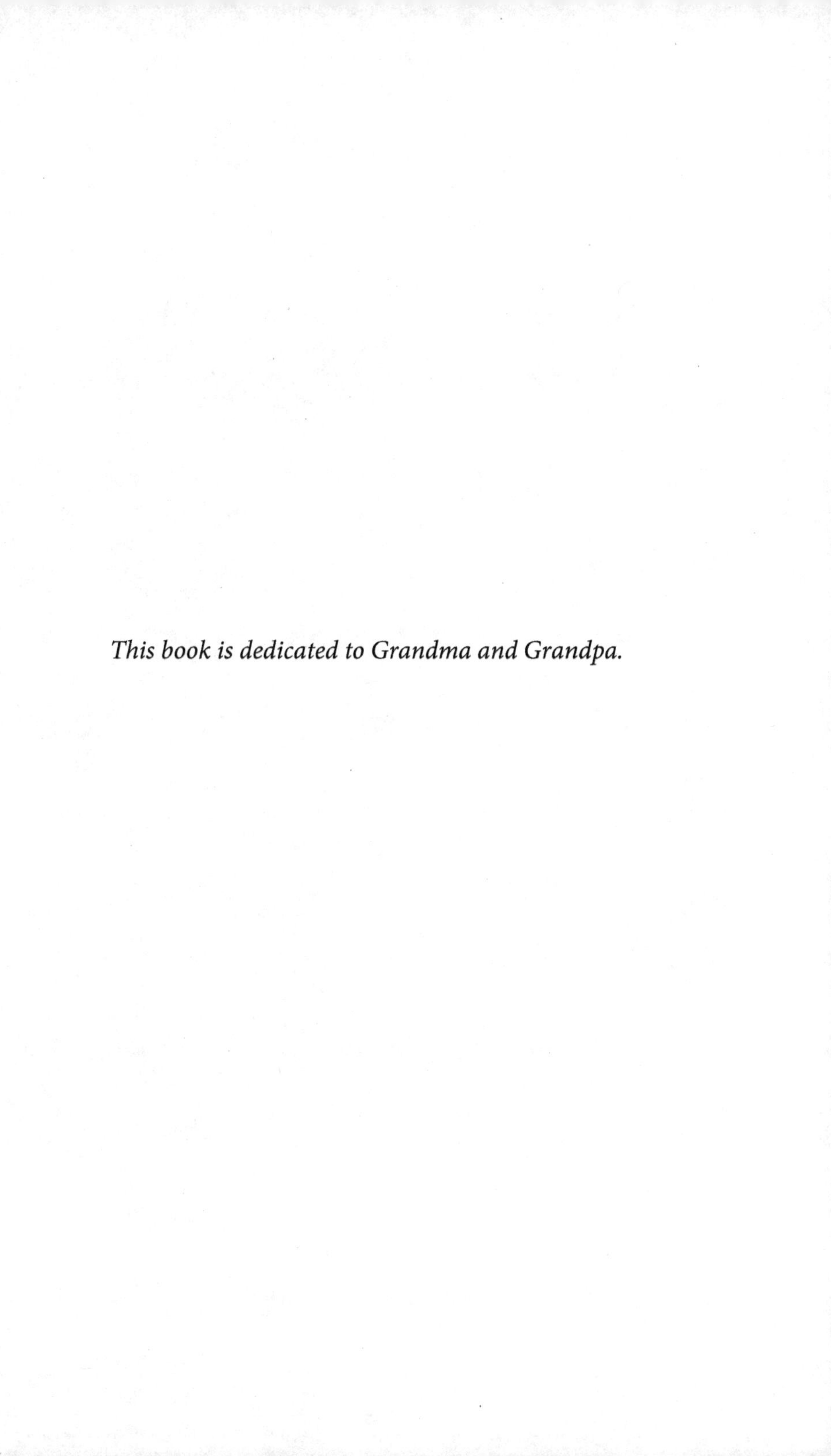

This book is dedicated to Grandma and Grandpa.

CONTENTS

MEET THE EDITOR

Aishwarya Patro

Aishwarya Patro, nineteen, a passionate poetess and a student of science currently pursuing her bachelors' degree in planning at Odisha University of Technology and Research, formerly known as CET.

She beholds a profound interest in literature and is an 'out-of-the-box' observer. She refuses to be anchored to the past rather learn from the mistakes, believing life isn't about waiting for the storm to pass but about learning to dance in the rain. Besides writing, she's someone with a fondness for animals and considers fostering animals as a lifelong endeavour.

She occasionally enjoys painting herself blue with music, while Linkin Park brings other colours to her canvas. She is obsessed with beaches, pebbles, and sandcastles. She constantly fantasizes about a seraglio next to a beach and being surrounded by flora more like complete mountains and forests and abstract art and sunsets and lilac skies. She is a sucker for countrysides, stargazing and a crescent moon. She is best described as a wolfy maniac.

'The touch of maple in early autumn' and 'The holy artistry of cosmos' are her debut poetries.

EDITOR'S NOTE

Like the aroma of those warm freshly baked cookies left on father's shirt for carrying it all along, for I treasured them the most. His shoulders would brush away all of my blues by his chest, watching me balancing on strings of black and brown.

I hold this book close to my heart. I enjoy the raw and vehement feelings of the words stringing together to form this amazing concoction of candid solicitudes.

There is no way that any of us is 'okay', and neither do I claim that this would make it better, but it sure would be like a warm blanket of familiarity and comfort, that we all live the same life in some ways.

Some nights with a plane enroute to my deepest feelings, I let myself put down my guard and breath in the bare adulation of my brain running from and towards the crude intensities and passions of life, at the same time. The indecisiveness of this action and the constant search of a 'home' by my mind and soul has, and by that of many others is reflected in these writings. We mortals seek solace in pain and greatly cherish lost memories, the past and the future. This looks at celebrating and validating, by putting into writing, the pains, and memories of our lives.

Down the lane, my close friends have been nothing less than a backbone, my family and writers who have been obliging throughout the process. I'd like to think of this book as a gift from all that's mine to all that's yours.

Distorted Reality
by Ayush Panda

The archaic minds weighed you down every day,
dulling your sublime young soul.
Draped in your sheets on a cold bed, you sway,
day in and day out, trying to make yourself whole.

It seeps in through the closed windows,
a faint sound of the rain.
The sorrow in your eyes that shows,
you entrapped life full of pain.

Every day, you feel alike,
a lost soul inside a maze.
A masquerade, that's what you hide behind,
your tears replace the blazing rage.

The cacophony of the entrapped mind,
quelled by substances.
They say, "Hey, try to be content, try to be kind,"
but your mind rejects it.
It shows reluctance.

You tread towards an aliferous light,
begging for it to shine upon you.
Hoping for it to wrap you in its warm embrace,
and washing away all your rues.

Your splintered heart,
it bleeds out a wicked dark ink.
Carved on your body, it gets darker every minute,
it toys with your mind, pushing you to the brink.

Tangled in countless dark dreams and some with a pleasant
sight,
you walk down a road unknown; you look very shaken.
Your gaze keeps drifting aimlessly, looking for some strength to
fight,
it's a birth of hopelessness, and you can't help feeling forsaken.

And one day you open your eyes,
the storm inside your head has died.
The warm hue of the morning sun drowns the room,
gone are those nights when you lay awake and cried.

The lilac dusk has replaced the monochrome days,
your heart has started to bleed red again.
The moment you thought you could never witness,
has come to you, it's all yours to regain.

You no longer scavenge the ruins of your shattered mind,
to salvage what's left of you.
You leave all the cruel pain behind,
you finally found a way through.

Memories Down the Lane

by Manya Kaur Khurana

Not like I know this time either, but certain smells trigger the most random memories in my head, which I thought I'd tucked to sleep a long time back:

Like while watering the plants on my terrace, on a sweltering summer afternoon, the smell of wet mud promptly sprints my mind to the long-drawn out exit pathway of my school, and then I can see myself dragging my feet towards the gate,

and almost eerily, I can feel the surrounding pathway.

The viridescent trees, the vibrant flowers, and the velvety grass, all of which start coming to life in my head.

All of a sudden, the smell from my terrace fetches me to that exact pathway of my school.

Like the smell of crisp, fresh air, on the sunny, early mornings, some days, take me to that ominously clear first day of my second grade.

For some reason, even though I've forgotten everything from that decade, I still remember that one day, the one empty classroom, those bolted shut windows and that melancholic feeling in my soul.

Like the smell of petrol at the petrol stations immediately takes me to that one car-ride home, where I puked all the way on the highway, and then finally slept in my mother's comforting arms.

Like the smell of freshly crushed cardamoms, ginger, Tulsi leaves and fennel seeds, take me back to my tiny hands gripping my grandfather's Herculean ones, walking on the long road that led home. I can almost feel the smile on my grandfather's face resulting from my giggly laughter and happily bouncing feet.

Like, the smell of cool, stale air of nights lit-up by the nitid moon, takes me to my grandma's village home, the crammed mud-coloured roads and the neatly lodged tiny shops. Even though I remember nothing else, apparently, certain scenarios are too well-ingrained in some corners of my mind.

Not like I know this time either, but some memories in my head are triggered by certain smells.

Quid Est Veritas

by Deepanshu Joshi

The low-key whim to jump off!
Of the tallest platform, beholding
a magnificent view to die for,
to run away, far from these rumours,
to a place where souls wouldn't dare
to hush and gossip, tell tales of
thy deeds – both bad and worse.

While sitting among your 'loved ones'
Sipping your favourite drink, enjoying
the slice of pizza with the most garnish,
watching same-old TV; it hits suddenly,
especially in places like these, and then,
you choke on that same slice which
until then, you had been enjoying.

Lying on your bed, too late at night –
late enough that it's morning soon,
Trying to find a cure for the chronic
woe and sort-of discomfort that
you sense in the air; not being able to
breathe and live, not being able to cry
or speak, even to yourself.

Watching the cars accelerating away
Into the close horizon-like avenues,
pretty much out of reach, they seem.
Standing there, aloof and disgusted by
your feet soaked in mud, ankle-deep.
The high skies also weeping over the
utter defeat of countless lost souls.

Standing in the dark, under the shower.
Head high, watching the waterdrops fall;
as if allegations blaming you, for all that
you didn't do. Trying to bury you. Yet!
You stand tall, against it all; soaked in denial
but also embracing it all – this feeling
Of momentary defeat leaves you broken.

Remember! What peace there may be
In chaos, hiding or disguised deep within,
probing into the concealed intellect of yours.
Disoriented amidst many crafty notions of morality.
Wrecked by lofty ideals yet tries
to make sense of any and all of it.
Poor mortals – always looking for a miracle.

Simple Pleasures

by Manasi Narreddy

Of all the things hidden deep inside me

In an infinite vacuum peppered with soft viscera and warbling
droplets of scarlet blood

I hold my soul most dear.

An old soul

That revels in the delight of the elementary in a world of
peculiar complexities.

The joy of a perfectly stained slide under oil immersion

Of seeing minuscule cocci in perfectly spaced clusters

Crystal violet, the colour of wisteria in full spring bloom.

The ecstasy of scented memories

Of the rich aroma of coffee in a quiet café

Or petrichor after heavy clouds let fall sheets of rain

And little bits of light dance in curls and puffs of silver haze.

An old soul so deep inside

I cannot fathom if it wears the face of a friendly spectre or a ball
of bright warm light.

So deep inside
It has lived for as long as I
Shooting tendrils of love and wisps of happiness
Into a void steadily filling.

Be No More

by Achyut Vaidya

I don't want to leave, not just yet,
I want to live, vanquish my regrets!

But it's easier said than done,
these voices, these murmurs,
ghosts that I just can't outrun,
they haunt me, they scare me,
in my head they are like a gun,
raring to shoot me dead,
Crippling me within, leaving me benumb!

This life feels like dark blue sea,
I swim through it with pretentious glee,
but the boulder lies heavy within my head,
I keep falling through the water,
slowly choking with despair and dread,
I merely exist, I don't live,
I exist hanging by a thread!

I don't want to live,
not anymore,
I want to leave,
free from the ghosts,
be no more!

The Little Girl I Lost
by Uma Bokil

There was once an angel
born with the heart of a lioness.
Her eyes shone brighter than a field of stars
and she'd smile with a child's innocence
and cave under the things strange to her.
How could she know
her strength, her worth at a tender age?
Oh, but she should have.
When she grew up, she was tested, and she failed.
She failed to protect herself; to fight back.
She thought she was being served what she deserved.
When the blindfold took off, she faced the truth
and the sad reality of what she had put herself through.
She cried, wailed, and ran away,
swearing never to pour the same love
in anyone's life ever again.

As I look in the mirror today, she is still missing.
I can see it in the blank slates I have for eyes.
I see it in the smile I've practiced for years
to fool the world.
But she wouldn't be fooled.
She would know.
She's a queen who deserves to be loved.
Now, when I see a ghost of her lurking within me
when I'm being carefree and myself,
I give her the love
I never could before.
And I hope that with time,
the little girl in me
would learn how to fall in love again.

Tacenda

The sonnets left wordless, matters to be passed over in silence.

by Aishwarya Patro

The vision still lies crystal in her soul, the eve was blurred,
her sight was full of chaos and smoke.
Within his heart, the sky was changing,
something was choking her,
smashing her down to the floor,
beaten by the thoughts of her own.

Leaving behind a world now, there was the crave for wilderness
as she watched him wither away,
while it was burning holes in her heart.
The time died in deceptiveness,
trying to tranquil her vehemence,
She fell motionless to the ground, her tears rolled down,
but why was she so bound?

The nights descended;
had it ever been so cryptic before for not
failing to let her be touched by the shaken timber?
The sky showered, something came by her,
she was struggling to breathe, but a tranquil hushed by her;
the night fell awash.

Oh, the scotch mist was sensed, feeling the cloudburst dancing
to the notes of her death and the drops kissed her burial bed.
Everything was drenched, the silence was fetched.
The scotch mist was now cooling the wounds of her love,
by the swords she once crystallised on her own.

The liquid fire in her life was now burning in her eyes,
hypnotising her to pulverise the vision of her heights.
How heart wrenchingly beautiful was her cryptic fall,
the sunset and the horizon!

Darling, the illusion has been whipped off her vision,
she can feel that chill in her sternum
and fleshes out love in his bones.

He cracks her open from her shell,

for the light to escape making her realise

how the world could be of so much awe,

The one that she never felt with anyone else.

For one last time, she didn't choose those exotic elegance,

but the inclement nightfall is what her abstract chose,

while her blue sensations were still painting the sky of his heart
cobalt.

Flying into the sky, through the welkin,

she knew no one could ever anchor her again,

for her blue blood was now flowing in his heart!

The Nights

by Dhrumil Sanghrajka

Have you heard of it?
The sound of the night
Do not fret,
It won't give you a fright

Amidst the shadows,
Is your brain calling?
Like waves on the shore,
Each thought, memory, and aspiration crashing.
Some make you think,
Some make you smile,
While the others, take you away,
Farther than a mile.

You yearn for something,
That lies yonder.
But why can't you achieve it?
Is what you wonder.

Provoked are your thoughts,
In the night-time.
And you care the least,
About fighting for the dime.

It is when you envelop
Your mon amour in your arms,
This is what makes,
Your soul is so calm.

The night is when
The lonely souls yearn.
They pine for their other half,
Alas! Pain is only,
what they earn.
On their own,
They learn to live.
With the seeds of loneliness sown,
They begin to silently grieve.
As they fall,
In the battle of love.
The wings of their life,
Start to flutter like a dove.
Despite of this,
A small part believes,
Their tree of life and love,
Will again bear the golden leaves.

Eyes that Kill

by Achyut Vaidya

My heart palpitates unconstrained,
as I catch her gaze on me unrestrained!

My eyes meet hers,
And with no caution,
My heart crumbles in tatters.

Her turbulent eyes,
like a maelstrom,
unbeknownst to me,
they suck me in!

Her fiery eyes,
like a wildfire,
unbeknownst to me,
they burn me within.

"Come hither," they beckon,
as I tread lightly
prowling around to prey,
to lunge into them,
consume the soul and flesh within!

Little did I know,
sinking in my delusion,
I was the doomed prey!
lunging to my death,
Soul and flesh consumed within.

Angel of Death

by Achyut Vaidya

Wrapped in this blanket of darkness,
Venomous voices creep in my rumination,
Casting me down into despairing submission,
Besieging my scarred head to regression!

Drowning in the sea of shadows,
Baneful brooding dragging me to languid depths,
Without realising, I run out of breath,
Drifting in the arms of the angel of death!

My Angel of Death,
As I draw my final breath,
Caress me with your lips,
Absorb my soul with a kiss,
Save me from this tormenting abyss,
Put me to sleep, rest in eternal bliss.

That is my dream!
I cannot face you yet, my angel of death.

Here, I lay empty,
Too afraid, existence petty,
A recreant, wallowing in sorrow,
Living on for another melancholy morrow.

Raw

by Ammarah Safaa

Word so harsh that we don't expect beauty from it
but all of us unexpectedly fall in love with
the fresh rawness of the morning dew,
the clicker-clacker sound of the rain that makes us brew,
the soul-immersing breeze fills our hearts with joy,
but we stay empowered by the realms that maybe
it's not something to enjoy.

The raw echo crept into the room
and tangled me in my own thoughts,
Now, while sitting under the tree,
with butterflies flying past me
I realise that maybe I am free,
from what they say or hear,
Surely that is no longer my fear.

Mortal In God's Disguise
by Tanishk Singh

Over he goes with a smile on his face,
Doing his work with perfect grace.
People see him, he meets their gaze
His voice is magnetic, he whispers in a haze.

Doesn't care about what people say,
Keeps all problems in check, at bay.
Begins his morning with a delicious toast
As the light of the sun shines on his face.

When the evening falls, so does he
Thinks he's God wherever he may be
Feigns a listen to what 'mortals' say
In the end, acts as he may.

The gossip grows, the news foretold,
'This guy doesn't have friends, truth be told.'
Alone, he wanders in the starry night
Far from touch, never in sight.

The gossip grows, and reaches a point
The God is stabbed, bitten, and raved alive
Wonders he, 'What did I do wrong?'
'I was perfect, what's with this throng?'

The dying God doesn't realise,
That he was a mortal, in God's guise.

Finale

by Ammarah Safaa

Such a time has arrived

when staying away is the sole option left to protect,

both you and me,

despite all odds and circumstances

even if the ground trembles,

I think of it as it dances

displaying no troubles

the world resorted to this foregather,

whereas I have been pursuing this for a lifetime altogether.

Was I protecting myself?

Or was I protecting others

From the truth that haunts me,

living behind the covers?

Let it Resonate

by Susprihaa Chakraborty

Your mouth suddenly dries up, and there's an intense sense of darkness in your brain. The veins around your face start throbbing, blood gushing through your body at a speed that your mind cannot be at par with.

The pace of your heart has never been this high.

You look at your hands; they're starting to quiver.

There's a sudden tug in your stomach and you feel a huge weight on your chest, a weight capable of crushing your soul.

The air around you is suddenly heavy, you're breathing lead and diamonds.

Why?

If and only if the good could have relieved us of all things that cause us distress! Right?

Now, let this resonate.

You see, new life, an infant with an undeniable twinkle in the eye.

A touch of their wrinkled, new skin tingles something within you. They fit right into your arms, and you look into those eyes staring deep into your soul, unfamiliar to the world outside. Their miniscule fingers wrapping around what seems like your massive hand, with all their adorable warmth.

You are embraced by someone you love; the warmth of them slowly drifting into you. The faint thudding of their heart is music to you and everything in you comprehends the language of their soul.

You have a sudden fluttery feeling in your stomach before you are just about to do something that has great meaning to your identity. You stand tall and do exactly what you had rehearsed for the past years of your constant growth. A sense of sublime satisfaction washes over you.

Would it be the same if you had no despair?

We often question and define life the way our windows have made us see the world. We frequently ask ourselves, are we living or are we existing? What do we choose to believe, you and me who have nothing in common other than this penned version of my thoughts? Me jotting and you sweeping your eyes through such perceptions of my mind.

Do we believe in serendipity?

"Whatever happens, happens for good."

To live or not to live, to exist or not to exist is a question that, again, occurs to the troubled half of us, who do not believe in serendipity. The ones who resonated with the despair, the ones who live a life to find meaning of what has landed them in a pit they cannot climb out of. The pit, with the same earth they once made a house out of, and in the nooks – stones that they used to hold on to for dear life when climbing mountains of challenges. The pit a few dug for themselves, or the pit a few fell into.

A few of us were born in the wrong bodies, a few of us wronged through our bodies. Unimaginable despair. The air around us vibrates differently, the tiny wrinkles on the edges of our eyes only exist due to the momentary joy that life bestowed upon us once in a rare while. The scarring events of our lives, engraved in the insides of our mind that only the eyes of our soul can see. Healed wounds and deep scars. These hurt in cold weathers and remind you of the agony you once powered through.

Aren't we special? Me and you. Me, expressing; you, reading, resonating; you, remembering the time you tripped on those little rocks and fell, how you have taken a cautious step ever since, even skipped above it happily, knowing what you don't touch would not have the power to harm you.

You have a hundred other people telling you that the world is not perfect. It has obstacles and you've got to power through. You have friends telling you to chill out. You have a dozen people telling you to calm down.

Calm down, amidst the storm in your mind? Amidst all the things you have been through, going around in your brain in the devastating sweep of a tornado? Calm down with your emotions tugging at those unhealed wounds?

I have such a tornado in my mind, as I jot these things into this blank canvas that is asking for more. I have unhealed scars that are making my eyes tear up again. But this time, I choose to believe. I choose to let these weights drag me down, just so I can swim up to the depths where I can see the sunlight dancing on the waves. I choose to hit rock bottom, so there's no more going down. How long will I gasp for breath? How much more power should I give to a mere organ over my soul and my very identity?

Not just the world, but even our minds are sometimes a dark place. Our brains put our souls in a cage, synapse after synapse. The weapons that have torn you, will not stop tearing. The air you're breathing will be heavy once in a while. You will certainly feel the weight over your chest at another time in your life. But the very idea that you have your scarred soul to walk you through another agony is beautiful! The struggle, the lessons learnt and the increasing caution of our step for the next stride, is beautiful! Do everything, but do not calm down.

We are nothing but our soul; our bodies, merely a structured framework to help us function in a society. Our minds constantly influenced by superficial experiences, making us believe that we of all people are irrelevant in this world full of charms. We are troubled, erratic souls trying to just be understood and embraced for what we are. But the question that constantly rings through the whispering galleries of my mind is, do we really know ourselves? Do we know what causes this rage within us when we witness any wrongdoing? Do we know what causes those tears to roll down our face when we hear someone else's pain? We very rarely do know the reason, and yet we feel so very deeply, and that is why my friend, do not calm down!

No advice will ever take you out of the pit. No words could ever help you breathe in an ocean you're drowning in. No signal from your brain could possibly make you brave through cold weather.

What will help is the courage and strength you gathered through these struggles.

We will learn to climb those pits we fell into, after a few days of helpless pleas. After hours of drowning and hitting rock bottom, we will learn to kick the abyssal plain to gain momentum until we reach the top and see the waves dancing to the music of the sunlight. Only getting a painful frost bite will make us power through the next winters.

In every one of your struggles the only thing that will take you out of the terrifyingly dark tunnel and engulf you in its light would be the aura of a better and stronger version of yourself! A version of you that powered through; a rendition of you that never gave up; a version of you that knew and waited to finally understand and resurrect themselves at the end of this tunnel, to fall in your own embrace.

Reach out for the end of your tunnel, someone is waiting for you.

It's All in the Journey

by John Solomon Arul

This very journal is living proof of everything I'm about to pour out from my heart which has moulded me for everything I am today, which hopefully could find that special place in someone else's heart that enables them to find themselves. Well, it all just started from the idea of my inner voice meaning something more to at least one person out there, to just know that as long as they hold on to that vision of their best ideal selves of who they really want to be in their life, which always seems to wait in keen anticipation, from wherever they are right now, to those steps required, those difficult choices, those times where you have to pick yourself back up and get moving because you know deep down that it isn't the place you should be settling for. Most of all, fighting for what you truly believe in, pushing against all odds to become that best self of yours, that feeling in your heart that you value so much that it's worth struggling for, worth being different for, worth being embarrassed for and most of all worth your conscious effort to push through despite those moments of doubt, disappointment, pain, heartbreak, and for the very fact that it seems worth it to you, makes the entire process worthwhile.

So, stop defining your entire journey on momentary emotional states during a single phase of it. Yes, we will have to go through dark valleys, face these giants of negative emotion, many a time even face ourselves amidst all the chaos of truly finding that person we want to be. In fact, avoid labelling these emotions as negative; we are humans, we're not programmed to feel one way all the time, it is what makes us everything that we are. So, own them, wear them as a crown, accept it with open arms, and show it what you're made of, because if you keep trying to avoid it, just based on how it makes you feel, you will always find ways to numb it out and distract yourself from what you're really searching for. At least for the fact that in this entire world, this is probably the most certain thing that you could ever call your own.

Like you already know by now, these things are headed your way anyhow, there are always going to be new challenges every step of the way, so it's really a question of what you're willing to struggle for, despite it all. Alright, Let's say you want to be the kindest version of yourself. Are you still willing to be that person, when someone comes along and treats you in a way you could never imagine any other person being treated like? They stick all these labels they made up on you, based on how they feel about your values, trying to pull you down from where you've positioned yourself with all sorts of destructive behaviour. How would you react to this? What do you think are the motivators behind those actions you just thought of right now? First of all, it mustn't be surprising that such people exist, and it isn't because people can be such jerks sometimes, it is simply because not everyone may value the same things as you do, and for a matter of fact, that's exactly what makes you; you.

By the way, it's also alright if you ever got the idea of slamming this punk's head straight through a wall. Sometimes that's what it takes, to realise that it's not the answer, doesn't mean that you're this horrible person who could never be who you imagined yourself being. Remember, you've just made an obligation to yourself to be a better person, are you going to let what you feel during one part of the journey take away all that you want. Let your reaction be a manifestation of the values you hold true to, even if it means that you've got to take the high road from time to time.

Failure is always a part of the struggle, it is what success can't teach us, it is to know exactly where you need to work on. It is indeed a stepping-stone to where you want to be. But make sure, you don't define yourselves with this failed attempt to be who you really want to be. You are not your shortcoming, and most certainly, the way you feel at a particular moment doesn't make you who you are. Are you going to let what others might think of it get in your way? Where are you focusing your spotlight? More importantly, is your light strong enough to shine past the familiarity of your past into the uncertainty of the future?

Well sure, the type of person you want to be must direct the choices you make, but it's alright not to make the cut sometimes, to feel insufficient, to feel disappointed, to lose that sense of self sometimes. This probably serves as the greatest fuel for change because it makes you realise that you wouldn't want to settle for where you are, which gets you moving, and you're back on your feet again. Once there's displacement, you start seeing that everything you need is on the journey, that the answers and fulfilment you're searching for are in the process itself, and not any destination or a particular timeline that you could ever think of, and most certainly not where you are right now. This internal struggle inspires action, which starts to stir up in your system until the choice to manifest who you're supposed to be is taken.

Wear your failure as proudly as you can; let it show you where you're weak, what triggers you; your shortcomings. Again, we are human; we come with faults, without which we lose the reason to live. And yes, this is generally followed by guilt and regret, and it's not because of your actions, or the choices made from your momentary state of mind. It is solely because you are not manifesting your ideal self yet. Again, this should not be treated as a negative experience as it gives you a clearer vision of what you ought to do to get a step closer to that place that awaits your arrival. Now, if you really think about it, this idea of you doing the right thing wouldn't exist if you hadn't taken the wrong path to begin with. It plays that much of a crucial role in our journey.

There are always going to be people out there who'll try to define and limit you with an incident or a specific shortcoming, with that one little thing that doesn't align with the person you say you want to be. Are you willing to accept those hollow words of accusation, which are often a reflection of their own self-worth, and sense of the familiar? Can you find it in yourself to keep moving ahead? Is the voice within which calls you by your name louder than the world's? Are you willing to give up what everyone can see right now, for something that only you could see for yourself?

Choosing to go down a certain path will always make you vulnerable in some way or the other. It is a price you pay for making any sort of intentional decision for that matter. For instance, you've always been this meticulous person, and your best friend comes along and messes up your wardrobe searching for something which was in his back pocket all along, moments before a big event. So, when you see these series of unfortunate events unfolding right in front of you, soon enough, you begin drowning in your thought, the only thing that you once took comfort in knowing you could actually control, seems to be crumbling below your feet.

Now, in this state of confusion, you start questioning other things in your life, which only makes it worse. Now, nothing makes sense anymore, there is too much stuff you "allowed" to get in your head, and you no longer can see what is real and what's not. That vision you had for yourself gets blurred by all these mere thoughts of reality, and so, in response to this crippling fear of uncertainty, you might not break their spine, but you might just spit out these venomous words that could go straight through their heart. Yet again, it doesn't make you this heartless person that you would break parts of your best friend merely by a momentary lapse of bad decisions.

What matters the most is accepting your flaws and removing this idea of a perfect man which is made up only in your head and get to work on them. Take steps to be that person you want to be.

Could you find pieces of yourself in these illustrations? Well, if you're following the strings that connect all of us together, regardless of circumstance or man-made barriers, of course you could!

Everyone is going to have their own things they hold close, which leads to different outlooks on life as well as towards others. While this one person thinks there's no place on this earth for kindness, the other thinks that it's exactly more of what the world needs. So, stop trying to compare your story with a completely different book, which might not even be in your genre, to begin with. Fill in the pages of your story with the ink accredited specifically to you, which is fundamentally a manifestation of everything that makes you who you are.

Just know that these are obstacles that are inevitable, only pose the question if we truly want what we aspire to be. It for sure doesn't mean that the life we want isn't going to come at a cost. The bigger question is what we are willing to let go of during this journey of ours which isn't meant to be in our backpacks.

If history has taught us anything, the happiest and most satisfied people didn't always lead the most pleasant life, it was from that struggle for what was worth every effort to them, that in the process of becoming their greatest selves that they found their true meaning.

Alright, to bring it home with another example, let's say you're this doctor who's got this inner sense of meaning to serve the illtreated and underprivileged, and you've got this opportunity to start a critical health care centre in a bleak and desolate area for a neglected community. Would you leave the comfort of your own home? Trade your privileges for another person? Drop all you're doing and seize the opportunity? Well, if you're playing this right now, you would unquestionably say yes without a second thought, because this is everything this person wanted to be. He would go and do it despite the challenges, the sacrifices, and struggle, giving him the purest form of happiness, which by the way, doesn't always depend on how you feel. You can struggle greatly for a cause and still be immensely happy, and it's not because he is sacrificing all those things he could have instead, but for the very fact that he is following the voice of his best self, which seems to be CALLING him towards his destination. Yes, if the word calling feels familiar, it's as simple as this, cause this my friends, is the story of purpose.

What are you willing to let go of? Is it that relationship, that egoistical sense of righteousness, those delusional thoughts you use to numb yourselves from the real problems at hand, the self-made pits of misery you drown yourself in, the familiarity of your past patterns? What's been holding you back all this time? Your best self is always three steps ahead of you, so get cracking, align your values, prioritise what's most important to you. This form of struggle is always a sign of growth and progress. Being dissatisfied creatures as we are, it's what makes us strive to be more. Fall, but don't choose to stay there and play the victim of circumstance. No one can do it for you. Let every emotion run its course, don't try rushing anything, stick with it, stop trying to cover it up or numb it out, let it teach you the greatest lessons that only that particular emotion could possibly bring to light. That's probably why there are seven colours in the rainbow.

By the way, spending time and energy to heed to the still voice of your ideal self is the most productive resource that you could ever spend. Not only because it saves you from spending it on stuff that hardly means anything to you, but because you have values so true to yourself that you would never lose sight of why you would do the things you do, and that every step you take has a deeper purpose. It's in this process where we realise that we all have different parts to play, which gives us this greatest sense of self, which dissolves all sorts of jealousy and self-righteousness. It Helps us appreciate every single person along the way, for who they are, despite their shortcomings, however obvious. Of course, sometimes it gets messy, you've got to reach down places and drag out stuff no longer fitting your ideals, which is always a painful struggle, but with the pain comes something beautiful, a new sense of self, which can be strong enough for you to handle any "how", because you know the "why".

Postscript

When I meant that this was living proof of what I wanted to portray, it's that there were times when I sat down to write what was on my mind, it was a battle of what I wanted more, the things I could settle for in the moment, based on how I just felt or being something more not only for myself but for somebody out there. To whoever reading this right now, just know that it wouldn't have been possible if we function based on mere superficial factors that are only going to keep changing.

What it just showed me is that on the other side of the struggle and pain, is an infinite source of whatever we're looking for. If only we could find it in ourselves to get back up and get moving in the right direction again and follow that voice which eagerly seems to call us to be more with every waking second, is that we manifest what we're truly meant to be, not only for ourselves but for the people around us.

I Called Home Once

by Harita Odedra

I could make a home of you
One day.
I dreamed of summer walks,
Holding your hand.
But it was you who painted the air
Thick in red,
While green bloomed in its prime.
I cherished my childhood
cradled in your arms, under the open sky
Feeling safe and quiet.
You let doubt creep into my skin,
Coating every nerve.
You watched in silence,
My soundless undoing.
You were pure once,
Your air was pregnant with laughter.
Now you have become a shell
Of what you were.
I am scared,

Scared of closing my eyes around you,
afraid of feeling safe.
Just to have you betray it again.
I once dreamed of a home with you,
But you crushed it with your fingers.
Years have gone by,
But I still
Tiptoe around the memories.
I have built walls to keep you away
yet you linger in the back,
watching me pluck out the bitter parts
just so I can breathe.

Dear Depression

by Sarthak Khurana

My sincere apologies for answering you a bit late, because somewhere, I was lost finding the ways out of the cobweb you tried to put me in. I had been wandering in the deepest routes of the thick forest of blooming hitches and the apprehensions going in my mind. And here I am, confronting you with all my will.

I know you love me a lot. You never leave a chance to influence me and show your affection whenever I feel alone. Earlier as a kid, I never knew who you were. I had just heard about you from the old fogey. They told me how you added to their lives by making them stronger than ever. I never thought I would meet you this early and you would become an indispensable part of my life.

I still remember meeting you for the very first time. Fall had begun, I expected it to pass away faster because I loved winter more. I couldn't wait any longer to finally get new woollen and sleep in the cosy silk quilt. That season did pass away quite fast, taking away with it the most precious person of my life – my best friend. I was sad, lonely. I thought no one could ever replace him in my life. And that's when I saw you coming. You replaced him. You became my best friend.

You were there with me, day and night. You didn't let me sleep, you didn't let me eat or do anything I wanted to. You behaved just like a loyal companion would do, always staying near to me. Eventually, I started thinking you were subjugating me in every aspect. That was the time I started thinking about how to get rid of you. Then my life changed. I moved on a new path in my life, leaving you behind. I made new friends and started an entirely new journey. And I was happy. But somewhere, I knew you were loyal to your place. You would return someday.

I was right. You did. You did follow me wherever I was going, and you did perform your duty as a faithful one would do. You returned. I asked you to move out of my life. I was determined this time, that I wouldn't let you come back and mislead me again. You made me think a lot of things I never wanted to. You started ruining my life. All you did was go away and then turn back again some time. I was tired of watching your pendulum striking my mind back and forth. And yet, you came back again. Moreover, you still dared to intimidate me to my worst.

You know what, I am glad you were there. You showed me my worth. You showed me what I was capable of doing. You showed me my weakest points so that I could amend them to my best. And I thank you for it. You've done so much for me that no one else could have done.

This time, I am sure I don't want you in my life anymore. I have those people in my life for whom I can die, those people for whom I can lose my happiness just to see them smile. And you, dear depression, thank you for not making me any stronger. Thank you for making me realise how strong I already was. Thanks for making me realise the true worth of my life and the people who make it worth living for me.

The Sunflower Girl

by Shreya Bhangare

There's a little girl I see every day with a smile as bright as a sunflower, I may say. She would walk along the sidewalk in the evening with a skip in her step, excited to be out; her eyes shining at all the little things she would see on the way. She would stop for a moment and breathe it all in, close her eyes, smile and let it all sink in. She would then start walking again. I saw her stumble on a pebble and fall down. That would hurt, I thought. But she just brushed the dust off her scraped knee, got up and started walking again. Any passer-by would think she was too happy to be out. A giddy, fairy-tale girl.

I saw her halt in front of an orange, one-storey house with beautiful roses, lilies and butterflies in the front yard. She fumbled with the little bow on the waistline of her oversized shirt. Did I mention she was wearing an oversized full sleeved orange shirt and equally oversized blue denim jeans? Who could have, when too mesmerised by her cheerful smile anyway? I saw her frown and hesitate as her little fingertips touched the brown gates of that house, just as pretty as her.

She slid the gates away and walked past and into the beautiful front yard, listening to the chirping of two mynahs flying up and above. I saw her walk to the deep mahogany main door and hesitate more as she fumbled and crinkled the fabric of her jeans' pockets with her tiny little hands before taking out the keys and unlocking that massive door. I followed her as she walked past the main hall into a bright yellow room. She was alone in the house. She smiled as she saw a newspaper hat on the wide wooden table; her best friend had made it for her when she had called in sick and didn't go to school today. He had come over to her house right after school demanding to see her and had given her the hat saying, "It will make you all okay." Silly boy, he had smashed his finger against that massive main door on the way out, too distracted saying goodbye to his best friend.

The girl laughed a little as she recalled the incident of that chirpy little boy. She walked to the dresser in the yellow room and stood before the mirror. She unbuttoned her jeans and winced as she slid them past the knees she had scrapped before. Button by button she slowly removed her shirt and dropped it on the jeans lying next to her legs. She was just in her little pink underwear now. She looked up and gazed at my eyes in the mirror. Clueless eyes with questions and tears brimming deep under. Why? Why am I such a bad child? Why do I just always keep being wrong? Why can't I be like the other little girls in the class? Why am I so ugly? Why at the age of 10 do I hate myself so strongly? She rubbed away her tear-stained cheeks, wincing as the blue green skin on her arms tingled.

She walked forward towards me as her equally bruised and swollen thighs screamed out in pain. The pain should have been unbearable, I mused; but she was okay with it. They did not hurt her anymore. We looked each other in the eye, trying to make sense of the situation we were in. He had called us a bad child, a mistake. We shouldn't have existed. He had lashed out at us. His hands, his belt, the cream-coloured plastic chair he uses in his study, we've felt them. We've felt them bite and graze all this skin on our body. Yesterday, we also felt the book he so lovingly bought for his wife scrape our cheek. He was right. We shouldn't have existed.

Yesterday was too much for us. We couldn't go to school. School was always a good distraction. We desperately needed a similar one today. We had sneaked into his study early today and spent the afternoon reading the same book he had thrown at us. It was a good book. It was a good distraction. We decided to forgive the book. It wasn't the book's fault anyway. We had arranged everything back in its place before we went for our evening walk. 'He wouldn't know what we did today,' she smiled at me. She smiled and my puffed-up, red, tear-stained cheeks stretched to form a curve. Uneven and swollen. She smiled once again and turned her back to me. Numerous red lines painted on her little back. She walked to the table, picked up the massive newspaper hat and walked back to me. I saw her put the hat on her little head. She smiled back again at me as I tried to feel the weight of the hat on her head.

"It will be alright our best friend has said," she beamed at me.

"We will be okay." She smiled brightly. I was happy about the distraction. Content with hiding behind that beautiful happy smile.

Ready.

Journey Back Home

by Shaymi Shah

"I thought my happiness left with you,
little did I know it was waiting to be found
by me, all along."

"I am finally home," she exclaimed as she entered the door of Priya's house. Raman Chacha, the caretaker of her house for the past twenty years, had opened the door when the bell rang a few minutes ago and allowed a young woman, who claimed to be Priya's best friend, to come in. Priya was quietly sitting on the sofa that she never got up from, except for the time that she had to make her coffee or take a shower or go to bed. She had a very loving husband, Abhay, and two daughters who were fond of her, Misha and Kriti. She loved them all dearly, but somehow never found herself happy in their company. It was as though happiness had left the station of her mind a long time ago and the train was never going to come back. She didn't remember when the last time was that she had felt truly happy. Was it when she got married to the love of her life? Was it when she won the award for the best woman writer of the year, for her most recent best seller "Left Without a Goodbye" which had deeply touched the hearts of millions of readers? Was it when she had given birth to her children? Or was it when she had last seen him, years ago, when they had met for the last time, before he left her forever?

Sadness, anxiety, guilt, and anger had found residence in her mind, far too long and made her believe that she deserved to feel miserable. She kept falling prey to the games of her subconscious mind, and nightmares that deprived her of a sound sleep. She knew she could never be with him again, and he still kept coming back to her thoughts in the day and dreams at night. The very thought of ever coming across him again, the one who had betrayed her, the one who took away her happiness forever, terrified her so much. Abhay, who had been very supportive, would comfort her and hug her while she poured her heart out. He was truly the best husband someone could ever dream of. And yet, she felt like something was missing.

So, when her friend came to meet her, Priya, without the least bit of surprise showing in her pale hopeless eyes, didn't recognise her. Feeling angst at the interruption of her chain of thoughts, she eventually got up and asked, "Hello? Do I know you? How could you walk into my house just like that? I am going to have to call security if you don't tell me who you are."

Her friend said, "Calm down Priya. I know it's been long since we have met, but you will realize who I am, after I tell you a short story. There's no need to call security. I had already spoken to Abhay about my surprise visit. He was glad to know that I was coming to meet you." Priya looked at her, cluelessly, but found herself calming down, and sat back on the sofa, lost again in her thoughts, or so it seemed.

Her friend sat down beside her. Priya moved a bit, remaining cautious from the intruder, who was supposedly her friend. She said, "You know it has been quite long since we saw each other. Didn't you miss me at all?" She looked at Priya, waiting for an answer, but no reply came. Priya's eyes were staring at the wall in front of them as though she was listening, but her mind was elsewhere. She continued, "Anyway, I have to tell you all about the adventures I had on one of the longest journeys of my life. I met so many people, went to so many places, while trying to find you. You were smart enough even when you were the most depressed. Remember how we were waiting at the station to board the train, and I got in as soon as the doors opened, but you being lost in your world of thoughts, froze in place, and let the doors shut in front of you? It was the last time we saw each other. You abandoned me on a train. I didn't even know where it was going to take me, and where you were going to go. For the love of our spontaneity, we had decided to buy the ticket to a random station once we sat inside the train. Do you know what it felt like when I didn't know where I could go?"

She nudged her to see if Priya was alright; it startled her for a moment before she got lost again. Her friend continued, "For two years, I kept trying to contact you, but it was all in vain. I kept looking for you, never knowing that you didn't want to be found. But you know me, I don't give up. I don't lose hope and I certainly don't leave people I care about. So, I had decided that I was going to find you, no matter what." She looked at Priya who suddenly looked like she was about to faint out of exhaustion.

"Priya, are you listening? Do you want water? You look so tired. What is happening to you?" She asked her as she got up to fetch a bottle of water from the kitchen. She couldn't believe how miserable Priya looked. They had been best friends since childhood. She was the one who made Priya feel alive and hopeful. Every time Priya felt sad, she would comfort her and tell her that everything was going to be alright. But what she didn't realise was that when she left on the train years ago, it was as though Priya lost all hope, making herself believe that she had to live without her company forever. She gave her water and asked if she felt better. Priya nodded in agreement.

"My goodness Priya, you scared me for a bit. Since when have you been like this?"

Priya replied, "I don't remember," looking at her with eyes full of emptiness, to which her friend said, "Okay, we will figure it out. Don't worry."

She continued, "Anyway, I met the weirdest people on my journey. They had the most amusing stories to tell. I remember someone jumping off the train to see if he could escape death, within a span of a few seconds. One woman in her sixties told me about her life, how she had been the victim of assault more times than she could count, but somehow, she had always managed to escape to hide in another place. I even came across some dangerous men who belonged to an underground gang, talking about the crimes and murders they had committed. I grew very uncomfortable in their presence, and I realised that the next station was coming up, so I got down there.

"It was so quiet that it seemed like no one lived there. I walked alone in darkness, slowly moving through the streets, using the dim street lights as my only guiding source. I saw a house at the end of the street, and I walked towards it. I knocked on the door. A young man in his twenties opened the door drowsily. I told him I needed shelter just for a night and a place to wash up before I left. He looked at me blankly, as though he didn't understand what I was saying, and closed the door on my face. I realised he was drunk. So, I left and went to the next house that I saw. I knocked on the door, and you won't believe the response I got when I told them who I was and how lovely it would be if they would let me stay there, just for the night. They said they had been waiting for me to pay a visit. How surprising is that, right?"

Priya said, sounding uninterested, "It truly is."

She continued, "Apparently, they knew about me. They had read about me in books and blogs on the internet. I found out while talking to them, that I was once a part of every ritual and celebration that took place here. But over a period of time, due to the attacks from the nearby villages and towns, people began forgetting about me, owing to the misery they had to live in.

"There was a group of scholars who had started writing about me and preached it to their disciples. They thought, maybe not in person, but at least as a myth I could remain alive in their minds. They told me, now that I was here, they weren't going to allow me to leave. They had to prove to everyone that I wasn't just a fairy-tale story, I did exist in reality. I realised that before they became greedy of my presence, I had to leave. So, once they showed me the room, I took a bath, freshened up, took a small nap, wrote an apology note for leaving without saying goodbye and left. You can call me selfish, but I was looking out for myself, and my primary goal was to meet you again."

Tears streamed down her eyes as Priya asked, "You did all this for me?" Her friend said,

"Of course. I had to make you realise that you weren't alone, Pri. Don't cry now. Let me at least finish the story." She pressed her warm hand on Priya's shoulder to comfort her and continued, "Anyway, I went to the station and boarded the train again. While spending time listening to the stories of my fellow passengers, I began thinking of other ways that I could possibly tell you that I was coming back for you. During my years growing up, one of the skills I had learnt well was the art of disguising myself. It was amazing how over the years, the practice had helped me to disguise myself not only as other people, but as an experience or as an object as well. So, guess what?"

"You know every time, you went out for a jog, and a gush of cold wind blew past you, relieving you from the heat?"

Priya asked, "That was you?"

"Every time you stepped into a puddle of water during rains, and the water splashed on your legs, trickling down your ankles, giving you a chill down your spine? That was me too. Every time you felt the warmth of the sunlight on your face when you woke up in the morning? That was me as well." Her friend replied and continued, "Every time you beat your coffee, the smell mesmerizes you with its flavour?"

Priya said, "I can't believe this."

"I tried to reach you in every way possible. I tried to tell you how I was around you, with you, all this time. All you had to do was look closely, observe carefully and listen to me reaching out to you. I was trying to make you realise that what happened years ago wasn't your fault. He wasn't worthy of you. He didn't realise your importance. He left you.

"But I was here for you. I knew you needed me the most. But you abandoned me, the way he abandoned you, as you thought I was meant to be with you, only in his presence. But I am here now and trust me I am never leaving you again."

Priya hugged herself, and for the first time in a long time she felt great. Her happiness was back home, after a long journey, and she wasn't ever going to let it go again.

Dancing in the Moonlight

by GR Harshitha

January 12, 2018.

After three long years of living in LA, I was back in New York, my city, a place where my heart belonged. To keep me warm from the severe snowfall, I decided to head towards The Coffee Club. This place brought in a whole lot of memories – the exquisite coffee, the warm ambiance, Mama Baker, and a bittersweet memory of a long-lost friend, Amelia Baker.

I ordered my coffee and asked the girl at the counter if Amelia happened to come there by any chance.

"Ms. Baker? Yeah, she is sitting on the corner table by the glass window," she pointed her finger towards where she was seated.

At first, it was hard for me to recognize her. Her long blonde hair was replaced by a pixie cut. A girl who always wore bright-coloured clothes was now seen in a rather dull, boring, and grey jumpsuit. She seemed to be busy typing away on her laptop, stopping at intervals to sip on her coffee. I reluctantly pushed myself towards her table.

"Hey Amelia, remember me?" I asked, with an awkward smile.

"Emma!" she squealed as she jumped up from her seat to hug me. "How are you? It's been so long. Come here, sit with me." She still had that sparkle in her eyes when she spoke.

It was the same old Amelia, the chirpy, cheerful girl everyone adored. She had lost her parents who died in an air crash when she was only about five years old. Since then, it was her grandmother, who was fondly called by the name 'Mama Baker' who had taken care of her. Mama Baker ran the café to pay for Amelia's school. She was a bright student in class, had an excellent SAT score, and got into NYU to study Literature. She always dreamt of being a writer and an author of at least one international bestseller.

"I'm good, thank you. I got a job offer here in New York, so I grabbed the opportunity and left my previous one in LA. What about you? You seem to have got your hands full. Working on your bestseller?"

She broke into sudden laughter, which weirded me out.

"A bestseller? I write fanfiction for a website, darling. Mama left me this café to take care of, an apartment right above, where I live now, so life has been pretty good when it comes to money. So, I just chill most of the time, but I work on this web series when I feel like writing. It has a pretty good fan base, so try to read sometime."

"Wow, a fanfiction, is it? Who is it about?" I asked.

She gave that childish grin, and I immediately knew who it was based on.

"Harry!" we both squealed together this time.

Harry Styles. He was our icon, our one true love. We adored him beyond words, and it was only him we used to talk about. The irony is that we both happened to lose contact at the same time when One Direction split up.

The next one hour we spent our time recollecting all the good times and spoke about life in general. Before I left the café, we exchanged our numbers and decided to meet up soon. That part of me that was hidden and locked away somewhere deep within seemed to open after I met her that day in the café. She seemed to be the key – the key to the past that I cherished.

That night, as I lay on my bed in my new apartment, tossing and turning without sleep, I decided to kill time by reading Amelia's web series. She had named it "Dancing to the Moonlight". She had a pretty good story; no wonder she had a great fan base. But as I started to read the comments, I noticed many negative ones – not for the story but for the delay in uploading new episodes. The time gap between some of the episodes was about three to four weeks instead of the usual one week. As I was scrolling through the comments, I received a text from Amelia.

"Hey Emma, I felt really good talking to you after such a long time. I hope to see you soon. What about this Friday? We could meet up for lunch."

"Sure, see you on Friday," I replied. I set a reminder on my phone and went back to bed.

Three days passed and it was finally the day we were supposed to meet. I reached the restaurant at noon and waited for her at the table. One hour had passed, neither did she reply to my texts, nor did she pick my calls. I waited for another thirty minutes and realized I was stood up, just like how she did three years ago. But I chose confrontation rather than silence this time. I decided to go to her apartment right above the café to talk to her. As I was about to knock on her door, the door swung open, and out came a woman, presumably in her forties, and looked at me with surprise.

"Hi, I'm Emma James. I'm Amelia's friend, and I'm here to meet her," I said.

"Hi, I'm Judy Marshal, Amelia's therapist," she said as she shook my hand.

"Therapist? Is Amelia alright?" I asked.

She sighed and gave me a faint smile.

"Let me explain everything to you down in the café."

What I heard next sent me shock waves throughout my body. Amelia had been suffering from bipolar disorder – a mental illness that is characterized by intense episodes of mood swings – manic highs and depressive lows. Right then, she was in her depressive episode, which was why she couldn't come out to meet me. I learned that Amelia lost her job due to this reason. She would be the bright, joyful girl for a few weeks, and then instantly, drop down to a very depressive state. She became incapable of pushing herself out of bed, barely ate, and cut all kinds of communication with the people in her life.

All of this information seemed overwhelming to me at once. I decided that I had to meet Amelia and talk to her.

"Well, for one, I know that no matter what state she is in, she goes up to the roof of the building to see the full moon," said Judy.

As I was walking back to my apartment, trying to process all that was told to me, I realized why I was stood up similarly three years ago. It was my birthday and I had come back to New York just to visit Amelia. We decided to meet up at a bar, but she never showed up. I went back to LA and tried calling her several times, but she had changed her phone number, the previous one showing as invalid.

On further reading, I learnt that one of the causes of bipolar disorder could be depression due to losing a loved one. I learnt that she lost Mama Baker a week after I left for LA. She had to deal with all of it, all alone.

All this made me realize that I should have tried reaching her more. So, what if I called her a hundred times, and left her several messages? I could have flown back here to check up on her. This guilt made me want to see her more, and thankfully, the very next day was a full moon one.

The next day, I went up to her place at around 8 p.m., and just as Judy said, Amelia was there at the rooftop, staring at the moon. I walked towards her slowly, not knowing how exactly to start the conversation.

"Amelia?" I called her. She turned back to look at me, perplexed. I could see that she had been crying. Her face seemed to look like it had aged, her hair was unkempt, she looked pale and weak, nothing like the Amelia I knew of. I ran to hug her and started to cry as well.

"I'm sorry, Emma, I didn't mean to leave you waiting for me that day," she said.

"Shh, it's okay, I know. Judy told me everything. I'm so sorry for not being able to be there for you when you needed me the most," and as I said so, I happened to cry even more.

For the next few minutes, we sat there, doing nothing but staring at the moon.

"So, what makes you come up here just to look at the moon?" I asked.

"Whenever I look up at the moon, I feel like I'm looking at myself. Just like the moon –complete during some days and incomplete during the rest. Shining bright with much poise and confidence one day, while the other day, remaining dull, staying aloof, and hiding away from others. I feel the same as well. I cannot change myself how much I try; just like how the moon is destined to change its faces no matter what. I look at the stars and wonder why I was not like them instead, staying the same, twinkling and enamouring all those who look at it with admiration. It is when I look at the full moon do I feel complete."

I held her hand and squeezed it gently.

"My entire world revolved around Mama Baker and you, Emma. After you left the city and with Mama passing away, I felt like my entire world had shattered at once. I didn't know what was happening to me. The extremities of my emotions got me exhausted, and only after I sought medical advice, did I get to know what I was going through. I understood that my intense mood swings would affect the ones around me. That was why I felt it was best to let go of you and live the life you had always dreamt of," she said with a faint smile on her face, but with sadness in her eyes.

"Amelia, if you feel like the moon, know that I will be your sun, who will be there for you no matter what, being the constant source of light and warmth. I will never leave your side. We can fight this together; you and me, against the world." I paused, and added, "And yes, against the stars as well," I said as I winked at her, and both of us broke out in laughter.

No problem is too big unless you have someone with you by your side, holding you tight and assuring you that no matter what, they would help fight your battles. During the pandemic, the mental health of many has been gravely affected. We never know what is going on in another person's mind until we ask them, and it is when we come out and talk about what we are going through with others, do we realize we are not alone in this. There will always be someone who would be happy to lend their shoulder for you to lean on.

Darkness Beneath Lusture

by Ankur Mondal

I walk past the lanes,

Invaded by many and countless times,

Still want to invade it in my own way.

Through the hours of darkness,

I emerge with my glitterati,

Leaving my surreal remark.

They see my pass by illuminating and hoot with laughter,

But they fail to see my darkness beneath the lustre.

Silhouette

by Ankur Mondal

Hey, sunshine,

When I stand facing you,

What follows is a shadow.

Something that mimics me,

Something that mocks,

Something that echoes my inner darkened blocks.

A shadow which is dark,

A dark reflection of my very own,

Yet seamless,

Clung to me.

What it doesn't reflect is my shattered soul,

My wrecked heart,

And the fractured mind.

If you look carefully to realise,
It's only you who created the shadow.

And here, the world just sees and admire,
My silhouette.

The Silence in the Room

by Manasi Narreddy

Orange sunlight filters through gossamer drapes
And soft cotton sheets slowly lull me to sleep with each brush
and caress of my skin.
My mind sways to an imaginary orchestra
Oboes and strings, an illusory bassoon
Just another figment, a spark in a neural network.
Because I'm nothing more than a warped shadow;
Lucent paint over a taupe wall
Bent over pearly frames and the jade leaves of an arbitrary
house plant.
A wraith in a polka-dotted sundress lounging in a wicker chair,
sipping tea from bone china
Each breath a glimmering cloud of velvet wishes;
An amalgam of unspoken words and hollow dreams.

Life is A Run

by Saniya Shah

Growing up isn't fun
You will realise,
Life is just a run
Nights aren't nice.

Sitting beside the lake
Seeing children play,
I remembered the snowflake
Made out of the clay.

Those play dates and fairs
And her shiny bright eyes,
I remember her with the glares
Unaware of hiding her cries.

Let me come with you
She kept on telling me,
A few more years adieu
Then together we shall be.

Years passed by
Time flew away,
Under the blue sky
I couldn't hide my greys.

Is it too late now
Will she be waiting,
I should probably bow
Before she starts debating.

I know all this isn't true
It's just a dream,
Another Monday blue
Time to go downstream.

Growing up isn't fun
Life is just a run.

Tagged

by Kashish Lewis

Whispers echo in the hallway
I walk by, pretending to be deaf
but whispers are louder with silence
So, I scream words of love to my mind
to cope with the hatred instead.

I can feel the harsh eyes linger on me as I pull up a chair
scanning my body hair-to-toe; making me feel like I'm naked
I hear those giggles and evil laughs behind doors ajar
but I try not to listen, not even if they are too loud.

I'm hunting for the strength inside me
I'm looking for something
that they can't tittle tattle about.

They choked me with tags around my neck
calling me ugly, imperfect and flawed
chasing and waking all my demons
I had just put back to sleep.

I try to pull out the obnoxious voices inside my head
with the little threads of love left in my palms
My mind wasn't my heart's puppet anymore
the strings had fallen lose from all the pain.

They sting me and my peace
making my blood cold and my body numb
I don't let them in but neither can I throw them out
and to shut this loud brain up in my head
I need the calm of my heart.

To break free from these tags
I need to begin right from the beginning
Begin from within
Begin from my very being
Begin from the love I need to give myself
Begin from letting go of worrying
about what they think of me.

I'm still looking at the sky above my head
I'm looking past those dark clouds
I'm trying to make my way through the heavy storm
I let myself be lost among the stars
only hoping to be found

Throwing away all my tags
now all I want is for my spirit
to be reborn.

Darkness Falls

by Nishtha Dutta

Darkness falls every night
My heart starts to sink
With the first sight of moon light
Thinking about tomorrow
How will the sun rise
Darkness falls every night.

No matter how dark the night
But with the first spark of dawn
Satisfaction fills my heart that
After every night there will be sunlight
Still the darkness falls every night.

Life is never easy, life is hard
And that's what I get from every sunrise
It tells me, as it's rising
Cutting the dark, suffocating clouds
Of darkness spreading light,
I have to do the same every time
Yet darkness falls every night.

No matter how deep the matrix of time
I'll rise up like the sun every time
Overcoming every overwhelming,
Depressing thought
I will soar up into the wide, open sky
Will then the darkness fall? Every night!

But pushing away the negativity
Into the darkness of the night,
I'll rise up like a burning flame of light
Still the darkness falls, every night

But I'm no more afraid of the darkness,
I know how to sleep in those nights

So, wake up and ask your dreams
To wait for the next moon light
As I've heard that every cloud has its silver line
Darkness falls every night

Not Enough

by Avery Brimstone

Have you ever felt like you weren't enough?

I had always felt a bit out of place wherever I went. But it wasn't until around 2015 that it took a big toll on me. I was around the age of eleven when thoughts of self-loathing and anxiety entered my mind. I had trouble finding friends, I was still settling into the life of having divorced parents, and my grades were getting worse as time went on. I used to break down, crying on the floor, thinking that this pain would last forever, suffering in silence.

It wasn't until 2016 that my mother noticed something was wrong and sent me off to therapy. Before that, I had spent so many months blaming myself for my problems. I remember someone telling me that it was just a phase. Just my hormones. Just puberty. That I was overreacting.

And I so hoped that it truly was just a phase. Because I wanted it to end. And I grew more desperate every day. I wanted those cruel voices to just. Go. Away.

I spent about a year in therapy, and I learned to conceal those thoughts. I learned to keep them trapped inside where not even I could hear them. I learned to trick myself into thinking I was happy. But every time I made a mistake or inconvenienced someone in the slightest, I would lock myself in the school bathroom to cry.

At this point, my grades were going up and I had amazing friends. But every now and then, I could still hear those voices. I hated them. And I hated myself for letting them get to me. I hated myself for every mistake I ever made. I blamed myself for things I had no control over. Every time we had to work in groups, I would get an anxiety attack. Every time I heard those voices, I would tell myself I was overreacting. Every day, I feared that my friends would come to me and break off the friendship because all this time they only let me stay around because they pitied me.

And by 2019, I finally managed to stop mistaking the outside voices of those who loved me for mere pity. I finally listened to my loved ones and stopped telling myself that all they were saying was just an act. It was hard. It is so incredibly hard to believe that someone else loves you, when not even you yourself can.

And around that time, I finally managed to get my life together. So many people think that they need to be fixed. But that's not quite true. Everyone deals with mental health differently. Personally, one of the ways I learned to deal with it was writing. I had been thinking about writing a book for years. It was probably one of the things keeping me alive at the time. I had a story to share, and I wanted to get it out there. I wanted to prove to myself that I could. But I never had the motivation or confidence to actually start writing, no matter how much I talked about it.

And then in November 2019, I finally sat down and started. And back then, I would have never been able to fathom how far I would come in just over a year. I am now working on a full book series, I have a short story published in an anthology, I have my very own website and many more things that I never could have foretold. A lot of different factors played into that. The biggest one was changing my environment. And with that, I cut off the main source of my personal trauma, and instead surrounded myself with my true friends.

Most importantly, I've found a way to process my emotions and not keep them trapped inside. I write letters to my future self.

Everyone has a different way of dealing with emotions. And I am not a therapist. I can't tell you what will work for you. But I want you all to know that you are not alone. And you are someone worth fighting for.

You are enough.

The Revenge of the Missing Boy

by Pratham Kar

The alarm clock struck 7:30 and Jay woke. Looking outside seeing the playground out of the four-by-four window, he thought how it used to do a number on him. His life everyday was like seeing him riding the sunshine. Today, after a whole 8 days of being missing, Jay had decided to go back to school. He had seen himself on the news and like some psychopath trying to fulfil his one last fantasy, Jay wanted to perform at what was probably his last Annual Variety Show at his school. In honour of his memory, his extravagant performance at academics and sports and partly for a chance of him returning for the show, the school had decided to keep his act in place. Though far away from the luxuries of his mansion, Jay had developed a sense of comfort in breathing in the rodent-infested hideout of the love of his life.

He would never forget the countless times they almost confessed and surely never forget when they finally did. Walking towards the bathroom of the crammed 8 by 8 feet room he stepped on the ring, maybe the last piece of what was left of his relationship. He sat down on the ground examining it, trying to polish it with his hands, and realised the ring had lost all its lustre exactly as his soul had, due to the events that took place that cold October night 8 days ago. He wanted to mourn that it was over, his teenage years scarred by the romance he had tried so desperately to succeed at. He got ready, putting on that proud St. Augustine blazer and the glorious prefect badge.

He was armed only with his sense of vengeance and the surprise that he was carrying with him against a whole town and a million questions. He sat on the bench waiting for the bus, the visuals of the previous two months flashing before his eyes, the numerous naughty adventures of him and his soulmate, how he would wake up to his cheek being caressed and the few mornings that they had together beginning with the sweetest smile. Disrupted from his chain of reminiscence by the sudden siren of a police car, Jay ducked down, covering his face with his hands; however, they had not come for him; from behind the bench now, he saw another missing teenager who had run away from his home being taken back to his parents.

It had become quite common for teenagers to run away from their homes around his town for when one simply could not escape their shell. The only option they had was to escape their skins. Jay, however, wasn't exactly missing; with his parents having the knowledge of where he was, how could he be truly missing? They had reached out to him on his phone and had visited him, trying to convince him to come back. Their stretched-out limousine, maybe, had enough space for Jay, but maybe the walls in their heart were closing in on him or that was what he felt when he declined.

The poor mother cried and apologised for whatever emotional sins that her own son was accusing her to have committed and had it not been for his sense of a black-and white life, maybe Jay would have melted. His father, the owner of the biggest rum factory in the entire state, the typical rich person that he was, had a lot of feathers of white in his beard, and Jay took those for his indifference to black.

Waiting for the bus, he was trying to understand when exactly all this had turned so bad. Was it the time when he brought Bhavya home for the first time, or was it when his parents found them under the same blanket? Was it when he failed maths because of Bhavya, was it when his privileges were taken away from him, or was it when he could not fight back? Was he really the spoiled brat who wouldn't take his parents' advice at life? What was it that had led to the events of that October night? Was Jay just a victim or was he responsible for what happened to Bhavya that night?

Steering away from the painful thought of his loss, he stared blankly into the bus driver's eyes who had now been calling him to board for a full minute. He snapped out of his trance and stepped into the bus and was set on his road to redemption. He sat down next to the conductor who, even after having Jay's face plastered in front his face on the windshield, could not recognise him. Jay smiled to himself, thinking maybe it's true what they say, split your soul once and try backpacking the broken shards of your past life on your face and maybe no one will recognise you. The bus was finally reaching his school, and looking out the window, he realised that after tonight, it was never going to be the same for him, but he knew he had to show the world what he was capable of, the one and only fight that he felt was more important than his life.

Sneaking into the school without being recognised was not easy for the poster child of twisted life, and if it wasn't for his friends, maybe this monster of a boy would have never made it. So there, in the coffin for the Prince of Darkness lay Jay Ahuja, alive yet dead as he was carried into the school right under everyone's noses. After a gruelling 50 minutes of playing dead, Jay had finally resurrected from the grave. Trying to put the complicated bits of his precise plan into place, Jay could not help but think about how cruel the act would be, is that how he wanted Bhavya to be remembered and was it he who was responsible for this master plan of shredding the emotions of Bhavya's parents.

Did he really have the right to speak the truth, and if not, was there any other plan that God had made to lead the people to catharsis, an end to this cruel chapter in his life? Deciding to go through with it, Jay put his contraptions in place, hanging from the top of the fly tower over the stage. He could not help but notice the true vastness to which he was going to appeal tonight. He was going to show the audience the opera of his life. Wishing that it was okay, that one must not pass one's life with just righteousness, Jay put his final knot for his final act, a scene that was going to change his life.

Hiding in the centre of the crossing space of the stage, hiding now in plain sight, just moments away from his performance, Jay was finally crying. He had never seen tears in the 17 years of his life always shielded from cruelty. He had finally broken out of his shell, and for the first time, was feeling the weight that he was carrying these past 8 days. The auditorium had now become noisy at 50% attendance. Through the hole in the old cloth background of the stage, he could see familiar faces: his friends placed perfectly at their positions to become accessories in murder, just waiting for the final act, the teachers, the coordinators running around on stage trying to put every piece of the show together and the eerie sense of tension that was in the air, total strangers holding pamphlets with his face printed on them, everyone waiting for this monster child who had run away, only because he did not want to obey his parents who clearly had his good in mind.

At last, at 100% attendance, he saw his parents, his mother still crying because of the questions that were being asked to her, hiding her face away in the coat of Mr. Ahuja who was looking around desperately, trying to find out what new twisted move his spoiled brat was going to play; what new shame he would bring to his family. Not moved by emotions, this was a new Jay, the one who wanted his revenge, even if it came at the cost of his parents, a true monster. As the various acts faded into the minds of the audience, no one could have anticipated what came next. The last performance piece organised by the brilliantly wicked mind of Jay Ahuja.

Everyone was on the edge of their seats, everyone eagerly wanting Jay's face to be revealed when the drapes moved away. However, he didn't; running the show with his replacement, it was as if the last attempt to lure this monster child had failed. The glorious act of recruiting Lost Boys by Peter Pan, Jay's adaptation of this fantasy story on Peter Pan where the green clad pixie dust sprinkling hero would fly around, trying to fill the cracks of every damaged soul. The music, the lights, the show had almost become an eyesore for Jay himself as it reminded him of his old self, the perfect boy who could fix everything.

Just as the final act of the final performance was going to play out, darkness swallowed the entire audience and then came the blinding light and the blinding discovery of Jay hanging from the rope with his right hand. He had come a long way to finally become a Lost Boy himself. Now, with a sudden shock and click, the projector turned on, showing the gruesome acts of 8 nights ago, when Jay, the football Team Captain and Bhavya, his boyfriend and the Vice-Captain, were caught in one of the more passionate moments of their romance. It showed how Jay could not save his Peter Pan from Captain Hook, and how, in one of the corridors of the massive mansion, Mr. Ahuja had shot Bhavya in his inebriated state, and how Mrs. Ahuja and the servants helped them clean it up after.

The entire ordeal had been recorded on the Ahuja's state of the art security system. The shot rang out in the hearts of everyone in the audience, scarring them for life, and almost immediately, police sirens started ringing at the entrances and on the ever-loathed loudspeaker. The Sheriff was declaring that they had the place surrounded. Enraged at this act of his son, Mr. Ahuja took a shot at his own son, missing him by a few inches because of the flashlights aimed at him by Jay's friends. Jay let go of the rope like he was letting go of a darkness inside him and entering into his Neverland, and just like that, Jay Ahuja became forever a Lost Boy at last.

Trauma and Past

by Manoj Akela

"You know what it's like to be groped by a man who is supposed to be your neighbour but is a sexual predator with a never-ending appetite instead?"

Well, if you don't, then you're exactly at the right place. In this story, we're going to uncover the dark secrets of a little boy who went through the same. It's going to be a frightening and nerve-wracking rollercoaster ride, so you better fasten up your seatbelt, mates.

Back when Mp3 players were a big flex among friends and we used Bluetooth to share our favourite songs with one another, back when school wasn't just a beautiful memory of the past but was also a reality we created for our own happiness, back when we could do anything and whatever we wanted and no one batted an eyelid for that, this is the story of a bright kid who was always fascinated by this beautiful world.

One day, a series of tragic events happened, and the boy lost his innocence and his childhood forever when a filthy sexual predator invited him into his empty house to consume the soul of that beautiful boy; the boy was never the same after that. He was so young that he couldn't seem to understand what the fuck happened to him. But the hunger of that monster wasn't quenched, so he did the same after a few months, but this time, the boy understood and was prepared. As soon as the predator pulled off his pants, the boy kicked him in the balls, rendering him unconscious and soon unlocked the door and ran home.

All the light, brightness and his confidence were stripped off from him and he was left with nothing but darkness and depression. Can you imagine an 8-year-old kid with such pain and grit? He was so frightened that he lost his voice; he wasn't even able to speak properly. He needed a guide, a teacher who could show him the way to vent out the anger and rage that birthed inside him. But he had to wait 7 years for that because when he turned 15, he got his first phone, and then he discovered Linkin Park, and then his life was completely changed. Their songs resonated with the boy's life perfectly. He was so influenced by Chester Bennington's voice, and I don't need to tell you why.

So, the boy researched about Chester and got to know that he was also sexually abused by his uncle in childhood and writing was the only vent for his rage back then to cope up with that darkness within. So, it was the day when the boy started writing, too, and filling the paper with rage so hard that even the paper started bleeding.

The boy was unstoppable after that; he jotted poetry after poetry filled with rage on paper. The boy was so in love with Linkin Park that he could have done anything to attend their concert, but he was from a middle-class family, so he decided he'll be attending their concert when he got older. But his luck was as fucked as he was in his childhood, Chester Committed suicide in 2017 and his dreams were shattered to pieces so hard that it was impossible to retract that feeling. He got the news via a Facebook notification. He obviously didn't believe that and did a Google search right away, but unfortunately, the news turned out to be true. He confirmed multiple times even after that. His teacher, idol, God, best friend left him in agony and once again naked to be consumed by darkness.

It is said that only a true warrior can master their senses and fears, so the boy decided to carry on the legacy of his teacher of words and emotions, but he was unprepared and was in dire need of a new teacher who could teach him the ways with words that no one in his age group has ever mastered, then came in his life the perfect candidate for the job, and he was none other than Marshall Bruce Mathers III A.K.A Slim Shady and Eminem as well. The master poet who uprooted anyone who dared stood against him and the boy needed this exact strength to cope with the societal demons.

He was so attached to Linkin Park and Eminem that people started calling him crazy because they were all about rage and vulgarity but to the boy, their words were therapy. The more controversial and out-of-the-box content he heard, the more he got invested in the world of words. He got his alternate reality in which he could be whoever the fuck he wanted and do as he pleased. He started writing again and he was unabated, he wrote so many pieces on pain, emotions and grit but people weren't ready for that yet, they criticized him for being insane and writing fucked up bullshits.

Also, he had several girls in his life who promised to be by his side no matter what but left him anyway; they individually devastated him in such a way that he was broken and rebuilt again and again, this may be destroyed his mental peace but in turn made him stronger emotionally, each of the girls taught him what he was lacking, he was learning from his past mistakes. He evolved into a superior version of himself after every loss and believe me, he had many.

Talking about the present, the boy is 24 and is living a good life, with a handful of trustworthy friends and is trying to write even more than he did when he was filled with rage and agony, he was turned into a spiteful beast. He hated the society with every atom in his body for making him like that. He hopes to write more positive and motivational stuff about his experiences in the past and lessons he learnt from them. Although eventually almost everyone left him but Eminem, he's still around and teaching him. He dreams to be a decent author and a good human. He went through a lot and coped with almost everything but his dead confidence. He's still building up the strength to talk to people comfortably, although he went through traumas and overcame them, but they still have an impact on him anyhow. He's only comfortable with the ones who are very close to him and whom he trusts completely, otherwise he's a dummy in front of strangers because he doesn't trust them for what the society filled with people like them put him through. He will always be the boy who was killed in that closed room back then, now he's broken but beautiful, he's afraid but protected and he's a monster but an emotional one.

Postscript

No matter what happens and no matter what you do to make sure you overcome them, no matter what you do to fix yourself, there's still a part of you that is forever lost. But that doesn't mean the story ends here, you would've been broken before, but you are unbreakable now because evolving continuously is the main ingredient to survive in this cruel world.

This is a story of self-motivation and learning new things along the way. The reason why I know the boy so precisely is because the boy in this story is me. If I can overcome my fears and monsters, so can you, and yes, the sexual predator did get caught, but 10 years later in another rape attempt, so basically the thing is karma serves but not only when you want it to, but when no one's suspecting. I gathered a lot of strength to put out this story in front of y'all. If I can motivate even a single person, then I'll consider it as my greatest achievement as well as my biggest victory.

The Voices

by Sourav Ganguli

He opened his lips wide, and a strange noise emerged from deep inside him, like if a solid piece of him had split or popped. What was it? Something screamed inside him, and it was deafening. His ears buzzed a static sound.

"Twinkle, twinkle, little star," "You want to see a magic trick," "What are you doing?" "...like a diamond in the sky," "Here, here! Can't you see me?" "Up above the world so high..." he curled on the hard, cold, stone bed with pain and he screamed. This was it.

Born with a silver spoon in his mouth, Kevin rolled in ease and money, his father's money. His rich industrialist father, who ran the show and puckered the white collars, without a care in the world, the system on his fingertips. If only it was as swift in his personal life as well. The drinks poured in his father's glass as fast as the money did in his pocket. It wasn't long before it grew to an addiction and tiny Kevin grew with it. His innocent eyes saw his father's hands change girls almost every day, and the fury his tongue unleashed on his poor mother… His mother, the one person who Kevin grew to love dearly. Because she was the only 'un-absent' parent he had. He cared for her more than he cared for his own life, more than there were stars to count and more than the grains of sands on all the beaches combined. And when his father resorted to beating his quiet, overburdened, suffering wife, Kevin could no longer hold it back. Each night when his father would beat his mother he would run to his room and curl up his knees and sit as close to the door as he could. Each night he would wait for the beating to stop and then he would land a screeching scream into the pillow with all his teenage might. He knew he couldn't do anything but secretly at the back of his head he was collecting all this angst, hatred and spite for his father that resembled the venom of a thousand snakes. He grew into a shy, quiet, people pleaser. He learnt things to blend in with the crowd, which seemed like more of an entertainment than an involvement. But it worked for him through his high school years. He had a fairly decent façade of a life on the outside.

Things didn't seem to change in his family even as he grew older. His 20th birthday passed and on the night of his big birthday bash, that his father threw for him, to show off how much money he had, he saw his mother being pushed into a glass wall. Kevin had had it up to the brim and he was as helpless as ever, but the hate grew with every passing day. That year something tragic happened. Something that he wanted but hadn't anticipated. One fine night his father gave his mother a slap across her face in front of his relatives and friends. That was actually the first time his dad had too much to drink and raised a hand on his mother in public. But at the moment no one said anything to his father. Everyone brushed it off. And nothing could piss him off more than that. Something ticked inside him. It was like he lost control, something took over him and it was blood in his eyes and blood on his mind.

After the event, he picked up one of the shattered glass pieces that were broken due to his mother being rammed into. He put it in a cloth and beat it with a hammer, banged it on a table and finally put it in a blender to crush it into as fine a powder as he could. That night he took his father's soup to his study. But his drunk father was too hammered to eat it himself. So, he spoon-fed the soup to him. Forcefully, some might say. The fine crushed glass accompanied the soup down the drunk man's throat. The fine splinters on glass started piercing through his GI tract. His body started going number than any drink could cause it to be. He started grabbing things around him, gasping for something to be shoved down his dried throat. His vision was even more translucent than before, and he fell on the floor with a strong thud. All while Kevin saw, maliciously, with peace in his eyes and calm in his heart. He gasped for the last of air before this broken, bleeding GI Tract finally gave up and the blind alcohol in his system wasn't doing him any favours. He seized on the floor and Kevin slowly walked over to him and did him a favour. He outstretched his arms and strangled him with his bare hands. There wasn't much force needed. He kicked and pushed and his fat, ugly face turned bright red, and his eyes begged for mercy, the same begging that Kevin saw in his mother's eyes when she was being brutally beaten up. And in that moment happiness rushed over his soul. His father's old body didn't have much fight to put up.

Kevin picked his cold, lifeless body and shoved him on the couch. And he left. That night he had the most peaceful sleep he had had in 20 years knowing that his mother was free from a monster's dungeon. The bare poison that he had within himself had been spewed finally.

A year passed and nothing happened. For all who were concerned, a rich, old drunkard had died a mysterious natural death. Kevin lived his life comfortably with his mother, on the drunk brat's money. But trouble soon called Kevin's happy town. Their comfortable life was soon going to be over. They didn't have enough money to continue living their up-status life and he had to face the real-world problem. He had to arrange the money to make sure that his mother lived a peaceful life and he sure as hell wasn't going to make the woman, who had never had a job for a day in her life, work for her money. He had already sold off his father's estate, more than half of which settled his money matters in the industrial market. Kevin didn't have many options under his shoe. He struggled to find a suitable job for a few months before things started worsening. He was getting impatient and ran for any job that he could find. Amidst all of this a flyer came by. They were looking for clowns, and it paid more than 3000 per hour. He was desperate and this was the only thing that could get him easy money. He signed with a company and started getting gigs. He used to dress up in a classic clown costume and perform tricks for children at parties. Once he landed a highly paying gig with one of the richest men in town. He was quick to take it and when he went to the party to do his job, it seemed a bit odd than usual. The kids were disrespectful and as scrawny as someone living with a gold spoon in their mouth could be. He began his act with his usual "Twinkle Twinkle" jingle but rather than the usual happy claps and giggly laughter, two eggs hit him right in the face. Tangled amidst the kid's behaviour and fluency of mannerlessness, he didn't know whom to blame, The parents? The upper-class society? If only he could teach them a lesson. But he needed that money. He gulped down his feelings and went on with his act. They asked him to do a backflip from the table. As Kevin stepped on the table, he slipped and fell on the ground and landed on his neck. "Ah!" These godless wicked kids spilled oil on the table. He somehow managed to sit back up. He still somehow managed to smile. "That was funny!" What happened to him next, he had never ever dreamt of in his worst nightmares. All of them pounced on him and started thrashing Kevin. They used anything they could grab, bat, sticks, belt and surrounded him. "Hit him! Hit him, make this stupid clown bleed. Now this is funny," the kids went in a trance. "Stop it you guys, quit it!" Kevin exclaimed in pain as he started bleeding profusely. Kevin could not control anymore, and he pushed one of them back with all his force.

Kevin was handed over to the cops. He was produced before the court, and he was found guilty. He was sentenced to 6 months of jail time. The thought of being away from his mother got to him. He could no longer take it. He began counting days till he would be out. On the wall of his cell, he was counting days in tally marks with a piece of blunt sharp rock. He would draw and scrap lines on the floor and the wall all the time, he barely saw the sunlight. His past, his childhood, his father, his mother and what she would be going through, all started coming to haunt him. Days turned to weeks and weeks to months. Kevin was losing it. His tally marks had gone up to a year in barely a month.

He opened his lips wide, and a strange noise emerged from deep inside him, like if a solid piece of him had split or popped. What was it? Something screamed inside him, and it was deafening. His ears buzzed a static sound.

"Twinkle twinkle little star," "You want to see a magic trick," "What are you doing?" "...like a diamond in the sky," "Here, here! Can't you see me?" "Up above the world so high..." he curled on the hard, cold, stone bed with pain and he screamed. Screamed, till he no longer could, and no one could hear him anymore,

His body turned as cold as the stone that he was laying on.

A Daughter's Guiding Hand

by Uma Ramaswamy

The loud screams of pain stopped 14-year-old Divya in her tracks. Her hands, about to push open the door leading to the living room inside the house, halted all on their own. She felt herself go cold all over. As for 12-year-old Shravani, her body began to tremble and shake. It was as if she was the victim, and not her mother, Sudha. Divya, the more controlled sister, could well understand her mother's sorrow and pain. She could even visualise her seated on the floor, or on the edge of the bed, holding out her hands helplessly as if to ward off the blows and abuse, with terrible fear clouding her eyes. After all, had not Divya herself, and her younger sister, Shravani, felt the strong lashes of their father's belt and his flailing hands on their bare backs, legs, and even on their faces at times, too? Whenever he was terribly angry, he lost control completely. The loss of control was even more if he happened to be drunk.

When Sudha had married Jayesh, he had been holding a steady job as a mechanical engineer in a factory. Obviously, he was well educated and skilled. Although they had to live in a rented house, the couple managed to live comfortably on Jayesh's income. For a time, they were happy, especially when Divya was born. Shravani was born two years later. Divya was delighted to have a small sister to look after. Sudha, of course, was equally delighted. To her, it did not matter that she had two daughters, instead of a daughter and a son. Unfortunately, Jayesh did not share this happiness. True, he strove to love Shravani, as much as he did Divya. However, the taunts of his parents, and snide remarks from a few friends, began to take their toll on his mindset. He began to depend rather heavily on cigarettes, as if all his tensions would drift away along with the smoke emanating from his mouth. His occasional drinking turned to regular imbibing of the spirits. He would sit moodily by himself, hardly conversing with his wife. Sudha could only look on helplessly, fervently hoping that he would become the old Jayesh once again. Nonetheless, she was thankful that her husband remained affectionate with their children. Therefore, their childish psyches remained unaffected by whatever was happening. Also, Jayesh continued to go to work regularly, and brought home a regular income.

As time went on, Jayesh seemed to be returning to his 'old' self. Even his parents and well-wishers stopped taunting and nagging him, noting that he was very happy with the 'gift' of his daughters. He began to believe that they were as good as sons and could do everything as well as boys did. After all, he was an educated person, and could display greater broadmindedness and intelligence than the ignoramuses, who threatened his peace of mind!

Unfortunately, good times don't last forever. Divya was about 10 years old, and Shravani, 8 years old, when their world shattered around them. They came home from school one day, laughing and skipping happily, only to find the house in a complete uproar. Their father was abusing some unknown enemies, using the choicest words possible. Their mother was trying to quiet him and requesting him to lower his voice. However, Jayesh was not in the mood to listen. Divya was bolder than her sister and demanded to know what had happened. Her question prompted her father to deliver a hard slap on her right cheek! Divya's head almost rolled back with the force of the blow. The unexpectedness of the action from a father from whom she had always expected and experienced kindness, as well as the pain from the blow, rendered her speechless. She could only stand there mutely, her hand on her cheek, and eyes expressing shock and horror. As for Shravani, she raced to her mother and hid her face in the folds of her saree. She was petrified! She had always been timid and shy in comparison to her sister, even preferring to speak only when necessary to do so. Divya was her self-appointed protector too, and could make Shravani be open, playful, and natural with her. However, seeing her elder sister become the victim of her father's wrath was too much for her tender heart. She began to visibly quake, hoping that he would not hit her too. Tears poured down her face.

From her parents' conversation, Divya divined that her father had lost his job. He had gone in for vile accusations against his manager for promoting someone else over his head. Jayesh had even raised a hand against his immediate supervisor. He began to hurl whatever he found near at hand, at Sudha's head. Then, he removed the belt from his pants, and began to beat her. Divya raced forward to stop him, but he did not spare her either. By the time his anger was spent, Sudha and her daughters found their bodies to be masses of painful bruises. Jayesh just walked out of the house, leaving everybody crying silently.

As Sudha had stated, Jayesh did find another job. However, he could not stay too long at this place either, because his temper always got the better of him. Therefore, over the years, the family witnessed Jayesh flitting from one job to another. He continued to smoke heavily, although his drinking bouts had lessened. His short temper did not remain confined to home and the workplace. It displayed itself on the streets too, while riding his two-wheeler. Arguments and minor accidents became a regular feature in Jayesh's life, causing his wife and growing daughters great agony. They had to face financial difficulties too, which only served to worsen Jayesh's behaviour. He never wasted an opportunity to point out that he, an educated and well-qualified person, had done the uneducated Sudha a favour by marrying her and giving her a secure life. If he had possessed good sense, he would have found himself an educated partner, who could go to work and supplement the family income. Since his useless daughters had cost him so much in terms of clothing, food, and education, it was their duty to earn, and hand over their earnings to him. If he had had a son, he would not have had to struggle so much. Thus, the emotional abuse went on and on, day after day, until the 'women' of the household learned to shut their ears to it and appear indifferent.

It was into this physically and emotionally abusive atmosphere that the two sisters walked into that day. For the umpteenth time, Divya wondered why her mother refused to leave her father. After all, their maternal grandmother was on their side. However, whenever Divya broached the subject, her traditional-minded mother would come up with various excuses, and end with "A wife's place is by her husband, until her death. I married him to be by his side always, good/bad."

Now, Divya was well aware that society frowned upon a wife daring to walk out on her husband. For them, the husband was 'king' in the house, and had to be obeyed and tolerated at all costs. The fact that everybody seemed to support him, had her hating her father all the more. The hatred had grown stronger over the years, making her sharp-tongued and bold. She would stand up to Jayesh fearlessly, especially when he tried to put her sister or her down or abuse her mother. In fact, she was so ruthless and uncaring with her words and attitude that even outsiders feared her. She had no hesitation in bullying people into obeying and doing what she wanted either. Her personality and demeanour began to influence her sister and mother too, albeit to a much lesser extent. Therefore, when things came to a head one day, as they had to someday, no one was really surprised.

Divya and Shravani were in their early 20s now, working in good companies, and earning well. Jayesh demanded and kept most of their earnings for himself. He was not working, declaring that his daughters were earning now, and he could afford to retire. One day, during a holiday, when he was out, and not expected back until evening, Divya made her plans. She rang up her mother's younger sister, who was in a government job and earning extremely well. Out poured the frustrations that had built up over the years, and a plea for help. Sudha's sister, Sangeeta had never liked the domineering attitude of her brother-in-law much. However, she had restrained herself from voicing her thoughts, because of her mother and brothers. However, her husband and children were very understanding. They had often felt that Jayesh deserved taking down a peg or two. In fact, they had also wondered why Sudha did not leave her husband. Therefore, confident of her family's support, Sangeeta did not bother to hold back. Boiling over with anger, she informed Divya that she would be coming over. Sudha and her daughters were to pack all their belongings and wait for her. She would take them to her large apartment first. Thereafter, they would hunt for a suitable place, where Sudha and her daughters could live comfortably. That was it. Jayesh never saw his family again. He continued to live a lonely life, living on the charity of his siblings, until his death 20 years later. His ex-family received the news of his death from Jayesh's siblings but remained supremely indifferent. They refused to attend, stating that they had no connections with him. In fact, they even suggested that his dead body be thrown out onto the streets, since it did not deserve a decent funeral! Admittedly, the seeds of hatred had only festered over the years!

As for Sudha, herself, she managed to get her daughters married and settled. Divya and Shravani, thanks to their jobs, were able to ensure that their mother lived in comfort and wanted for nothing. Even now, despite being in different cities, they (along with their husbands), kept in regular touch. They were glad that things had worked out, without them having to take legal help. As for Sudha, herself, she would not be human if she did not think of her husband sometimes. Regardless, she did not regret her freedom, for - "Never forget that walking away from something unhealthy is brave, even if you stumble a little on your way out of the door."

Life

by Nishtha Dutta

Life is like a mountain
High, steep and rocky
As we stand down hill
Fear rules our minds
Of what bad might
next be waiting

Let me tell you
Life is like a bad breath,
Bad experience may be
A nightmare you will sometimes
struggle to break free.

Life will be like the road less travelled
You will seldom know which one to choose
The travelled straight one,
Or the moss covered crooked one
Sometimes it will be nothing
But just standstill at a crossroad

Life will be full of thrilling uncertainties
Brimming with exacerbating circumstances
It will keep on getting complex
It will keep coming back for you
To make the climb

You will often have no choice,
Step by step the climb you have begin
Slowly, slowly you will start cutting
The path, make your own way
You will fall several times
But jump off those big rocks,

Dive through those cavy roads
You will reach high
When you reach the top,
What do you see?
You see a cliff and now
Nothing but to jump off the cliff

You will be scared and sit there,
Till the infinity, deciding either
To jump or go back
The irony; jumping down or walk downhill
In both the cases life's taking you down

But it's us, who will decide
Whether we want to jump in the water
The blue of heaven
Or to start the walk to go down
To the black choking hell

Decisions is what life is about
Correct or wrong, that's the tricky part
Avoiding it have never been the solution
What do we do in this life?
I choose the hard way,
I will take that leap of faith.

Let's not wait,
Let's not be afraid
Let's jump, for we might fly.

To Whom I Can Be More than One
by Ankur Mondal

On a scorching summer,

I can make you feel the winter shivers;

I, your man, a poet, can make you surmise.

On a dry and humid day,

I can make you feel the rains;

I, your man, a rhymester, can make you imagine.

On a boring and dull day,

I can make you travel a thousand miles;

I, your man, a globetrotter, can make you go places.

When you are blank,

I can draw you realities which will be endless;

I, your man, a painter, have the power to create.

On a not-so-good day, when you want to give up on life,

I can talk to you all night and recoup you believe;

I, your man, a partner, can calm you in your grief.

When you feel the world has forgotten us,
I will write and chant to the universe;
I, your man, a singer, will make us immortal.

When I become reluctant and torpid,
Your love stimulates the individual in me;
You, my man, make me what I always want to be.

The Yacht

by Tanishk Singh

My mind is incapable of

Taking tensions of trifles

Yet the yacht that sails in the vast

Ocean that meets the shore

Sorely messes with the aesthetic appeal

Of the whole scene

Where the yacht is sticking out

Like a thumb gone sore

How I wish I could just bore a hole

In the floor

And let it sink

Let me sink

Let me close my eyes

And for one last time

Enjoy the scenery without any yachts in sight.

City Lights

by Toshali Pattnaik

Flickering at a distance,
It captivates my attention,
Throwing me in pools of nostalgia,
It casts a numbing sensation.

What is it about city lights,
What story do they hide,
With their tremulous reflections,
In the river swelling in pride.

Gushing through my veins,
I feel a warmth in my heart,
Cause, the traffic fails to hide,
The peace of the lighted boulevard.

Though far away,
They comfort me enough,
Filling me with courage,
And the strength to stay tough.

They listen to the whispers,
Of every passer-by,
And hold them in their light,
Without letting out a cry.

As the ages roll by,
They spend their youth,
Sleuthing in the darkness,
The silent beholders of truth.

Yet they shower wisdom,
In their own remarkable sleight,
Beaming through the night,
The distant city lights.

Living the Nightmare

by Tanishq Malik

I shrieked in the middle of nowhere and suddenly found myself panting on my bed. On hearing, my mother rushed into my room and comforted me, making me reassured that it was just a nightmare, which was again hard to digest due to my psychological wellbeing. I as a 13-year-old kid suffered from Dream-Reality Confusion (DRC), a symptom of borderline personality disorder.

Soon, my mother left to go shopping at a nearby market, while I had my lunch and retired to bed. I fell asleep real soon. After an hour or two, I woke up on my bed and heard strange clattering round the living room. I took a little courage to look around the place and was spooked till my toe when I saw a strange man-like figure in black wearing a vicious mask with a butcher's knife! I screamed and rushed to the kitchen and hid myself in a cupboard.

It was five minutes and there was no movement. I crawled out of my hiding place and escaped through the kitchen window, but while doing so, I wounded my left knee. Without wasting any time, I rushed towards my neighbour's place. They were an old couple and our family friends, too. The door of their house was a little ajar; I peeked and soon, was inside the house. As soon as I entered the hallway, I saw the body of the uncle on the floor brutally beaten and in front of me was standing the same blood-red figure with the knife who grabbed the aunt from behind and in no time slit her throat! I hollered at the dreadful scene, and I passed out at the spot.

Next, I woke up on my bed panting and sweating, my mother was in my room sitting beside me and asked me, "Was it another nightmare dear?" I nodded to her unwillingly and soon she went to get me a glass of water. I got up from my bed but felt a burning sensation on my left knee. When I examined it, I saw the same bruise that I had in my dreadful dream. At that moment I heard the cops' siren wailing at the street corner. I was thrilled in horror and just knew one thing that *it was not another nightmare!*

Take Me Back
by Rafiya Tasneem

Places where there once was the crisp of leaves as we walked,
There was a faint fragrance of yours and some of mine,
I can no longer feel your touch in that sunshine,
Now the dusk is more comforting than the twilights.

Our sundering was now breathing down my neck,
It's been too cold in that fall, but it can't seem to freeze me at all.
Now this actuality seems much more apropos than my
deception.

Darling the serenity I once been bestowed by your affection
has now perished the sanity off my heart.

The Inner Voice

by Poornima V Krishnan

"So, how did this start?" the psychiatrist asked, staring at Ananya with curiosity. Before she could answer, her dad intervened, "Doctor, she is constantly anxious. She continuously monitors her pulse every moment." Ananya looked down as her dad explained.

Ananya was an IT employee and was working for one of the most influential software giants in the world. Curious by nature, she constantly strived for victory in her life. She completed her engineering from a Tier 1 college and got placed immediately after her graduation. For the teaching staff, she was the intelligent one who would go beyond a threshold and make a win.

After a pause, the doctor asked her parents to wait outside the cabin. He wanted to dwell on her past, which was usually called "counselling" among medicos. As directed, her parents got up and left.

"So Ananya, what a great name. Any thoughts on what your name signifies?"

"I don't know. I was never keen to know it", Ananya responded, disinterested.

"Well, the meaning is you are unique. And yes, I am sure you are. So, what are you scared of, Ananya? What is making you anxious?"

"Death," she replied, tears rolling down her eyes. "I am afraid of death."

"Everyone is. It's an unknown territory," the doctor responded.

"But there is an issue with my heart which I spotted lately. I had severe palpitations one night after work. I thought my day had come. The next day, we took an ECG, and the result showed variations. All the symptoms I have match with a heart attack. I googled it all," she cried out and gasped for breath.

"I'm seeing your medical reports. It is normal to have this. You don't even require treatment for this. Trust me. Are you still confused why you are meeting a psychiatrist instead of a cardiac? It is because your heart is doing fine. It is beating for you to make you feel oxygenated," the doctor replied comfortingly. Ananya looked at him in disbelief. She had 10-15 panic attacks a day.

The doctor understood she didn't believe a word of what he said. He continued, "Are there any other significant changes in your life apart from this health anxiety? Or to put it in a better way, ever been through this same cycle in the past?"

"No," she replied abruptly.

"Okay… Well, stop googling. I know it has all the answers in the world but not an MBBS degree. So, what do you feel when you are anxious?"

"Heart pounding, chest tightness as if an elephant is sitting on it, nausea, sweating... I can go on. It is terrible, and I cannot emphasise this enough. I see vivid dreams. Even in my sleep, I am anxious. I cannot suppress it at any time of the day. It has started affecting my work", she answered.

He was listening carefully, then moved forward from his chair and kept his hands on the table, and asked, "What were the dreams you saw?"

Ananya recollected the most terrible dream she had in recent times. She made her position comfortable and started, "I was sleeping in a very dark room. I woke up in my dream, and I slipped down to a tunnel. It had many side-pocket rooms. I decided to explore, still baffled by what was happening. In one of the rooms, I was talking to my old friend with whom I didn't have a good past. She had given me the most painful memory, but in the dream, I was talking merrily with her. I shut the door. I saw all the important people in my life in front of me moving around without even recognising me. I cried for help to get out of the tunnel. I couldn't move. It was one of the most mysterious dreams I have had lately. I perceived the dream as being in a strange environment away from my kith and kin." After she completed the narration, she drank a glass of water immediately and exhaled.

"So, the girl you were mentioning in the dream. Who was she? What happened to her?" the doctor asked.

"I had… I had been through depression a few years back," Ananya said, reminiscing the past which she never wanted to. "She was my best friend. We were like sisters, close. I was in a relationship with someone, and he cheated on me with her. I couldn't take it, and I felt my world crumbling into pieces. There is no contact with them now. After that, I was depressed. I looked malnourished and have had sleepless nights."

"Have you forgiven them?"

"No. Who on earth will forgive this?"

"I agree. It is ridiculous and what happened to you was disturbing and painful. No one can forgive at that moment. But why are you still carrying that emotional burden with you? You cannot afford negative thoughts that kill the riches of your mind, body, soul."

"But my anxiety has nothing to do with this story. That was my past."

"Well, to answer that, it's funny how our mind works. The past has a major role in our lives. Otherwise, you wouldn't have dreamt that now. You are still wounded from those memories. You have to forgive and make peace with it. Let's do a forgiveness meditation in the next session," he said affirmatively.

*****

"Now, you can slowly open your eyes," the doctor said.

After the forgiveness meditation, where she had thrown all her thoughts and grief away, Ananya felt happy. She made peace with her taunting memories. But still, she was not able to relate her past with the current situation.

"Doctor, I'm over it. Trust me. But how is it related to my anxiety?"

"I knew you would ask this. You know, sometimes you need not connect the dots. Few thoughts you should leave as they are. You get chest pain, then you google it and immediately connect it as a heart problem. Same here as well, you had been in depression before, so it is just an added flavour to your present situation. It's a funny thought, but depression, anxiety are all siblings from a common ancestor. You had one, so the other came to meet his brother," the doctor laughed.

"That's a funny thought. Wow! I never thought it this way," she responded with a smile that had faded away.

After letting out all her fears, Ananya was keener to meet her lifesaver. Weeks went on with different sessions and it came to a day when it was the last.

"So, this is my last session?" she asked.

"Yes, this is your last session. You don't need me anymore. You have proved you are not your anxiety."

"But how do you I'm doing?"

"Ananya, you are a brave girl. You have outpowered your inner voice. Anxiety is like an inner voice that you are carrying along with you. It will judge you, criticise you, scare you from everything. But you are never anxious. It's just an imagined reality. It's difficult to understand what you are anxious about, and we doctors call it the root of the problem. Stop connecting dots and leave it as it is. Whatever is yours will eventually come. Don't wait for the fruits of your actions, rather trust the process and move on. Never let negativity rob your mind because our minds are quite similar to the Ludo game. The different colours being different thoughts, one thought cutting the other. You have to roll your dice to make your goals a reality just as we get the pawns in Ludo home. And cut your negative thoughts immediately. Trust me. It works. So, keep rolling the dice and guess what, you won," the doctor responded.

Ananya began to learn how to control her thoughts, and what thoughts could do to a person. From then on, she lived with affirmations that kept her sane. She is not her anxiety anymore. She will never be.

Losing the Plot

by Joe King

Martha was sitting on a bench overlooking the beach, waiting for her husband, Carl, to arrive for their late-night picnic. It was early spring, and the sun was beginning to set. Carl was already ten minutes late as his boss had phoned in sick that day, leaving Carl to lock up at the hardware store. Carl had messaged Martha earlier to explain the situation. They had decided to meet down at the beach in order to save some time. Carl still had not arrived, so Martha got up from the bench and moved to a secluded beauty spot, just in front of a big, green oak tree. From there she could see the waves crashing against the rocks and the sun reflecting off the sea. Martha began unpacking the food from the picnic basket to be prepared for when Carl arrived.

As she was unpacking the sausage rolls, she heard a heavy, rustling noise from the tree behind her. It sounded like someone was shaking that tree. Martha ignored it at first, thinking it was just a bird or a squirrel, but the rustling became more insistent. She turned around to look, but no one was there. "It can't be Carl, as he is not coming from that direction," thought Martha. After a few seconds, as she turned away a fir cone came flying past her.

"Who's there?" she shouted as she turned around.

Martha waited for an answer, but there was no reply. She picked up the cheese knife and headed towards the tree. As Martha got closer to the tree, a man jumped out at her.

"Gotcha!" shouted the man, as he grabbed Martha. It was her husband.

"Oh Carl, you scared the life out of me!" Martha gasped, as she dropped her makeshift weapon.

Carl was lucky that Martha had not stabbed him with it. "Sorry babe, I just couldn't help myself," he said, while laughing his head off.

"You're lucky I didn't stab you!" replied Martha as she picked it up off the ground.

Carl had not realised how scared Martha actually was, but he soon realised it had been a bad idea to scare a woman alone on a darkening evening. It transpired that Carl had been unable to find a parking space, so he had left the car on an alternate road which brought him in from the different direction near the tree he was hiding behind.

Carl looked at Martha and then apologised again. "I'm so sorry, babe, I didn't mean to frighten you that much." Martha just gave him a big hug and said, "I'm just glad it was you darling," as she squeezed him tightly.

"C'mon, I've set up the hamper, let's go eat," said Martha.

"Indeed, I'm starving," replied Carl.

Martha and Carl started tucking into their food as the sun began to set. It was such a perfect evening for a romantic picnic. The champagne was flowing, the candles were out and there was not another soul in sight. All they could hear was the birds chirping in the trees and the waves crashing against the rocks. After a good meal and a few glasses of champagne, Martha and

Carl wrapped themselves up together in a thick, warm blanket. Soon after they did, the lovemaking began and that capped off a perfect evening for them.

The next day, back at home, Martha and Carl were lying in bed together. Carl woke up first and attempted to put his hand on Martha's shoulder. Just as he was about to do so, she opened her eyes and yelled "Don't you dare, Carl!"

Carl was a little bit bewildered by Martha's reaction. "What's the matter babe?" asked Carl as he pulled his hand away.

Martha gave Carl a filthy look and said, "You may have frightened me yesterday, but I won't stand for it today," as she turned over and tucked herself back under the blanket.

"What do you mean?" asked Carl. "I wasn't trying to frighten you, I was only attempting to wake you up, as it's 7 a.m. already," he said.

"7 a.m.?" yelled Martha. "I'm late! Why did you not wake me up earlier?" she hollered at Carl, who was even more bewildered but only because Martha had not long just berated him for attempting to wake her. He was feeling very confused.

"Babe, I'm sorry…" Carl began.

"Don't give me your half-ass sorry," Martha bellowed at him, interrupting him in the process. "I'm late and it's all your fault. You bought that big bottle of champagne and got me drunk last night JUST so you could take advantage of me again," Martha shouted at Carl. "I've been warned about this before," she then added.

"By whom?" asked Carl.

"Oh… never mind" replied Martha as she rushed to the bathroom with her makeup bag.

Carl did not probe any further. He did want to find out who had been bad mouthing him, but he also had no wish to antagonise Martha any further, so he kept quiet while she got herself ready for work. Martha then stormed out of the house, slamming the door in the process which made Carl jump. The whole house rattled.

Martha was in a foul mood. Carl initially thought it might be a hangover from the champagne they were drinking the previous night, but as the months went by, it became clear that this was not the case. Martha became very unstable. She would shout at Carl, twist his words, and hit him. She even called the police, accusing him of attempted rape when Carl had not given Martha so much as a hug or a kiss.

Martha had progressively changed since the night of their picnic. She repeatedly told Carl that she felt he had taken advantage of her that night. Since then, things had started going downhill very rapidly between them. Carl and Martha seemed to be growing apart. Martha would distance herself from Carl. She spent many nights away from the house, staying with her mother, Mildred, instead. Mildred was lonely as her husband of thirty-seven years, Frank, had been sentenced to ten years in prison for abusing and raping Mildred on numerous occasions.

This affected Martha really badly, and as a result, she was taking things out on Carl because of what her father had done to her mother. Mildred could not trust any man after what had happened with Frank, and she would tell Martha that all men were evil, and Carl was no exception. Mildred used to like Carl, but since Frank had started abusing her, she had turned on Carl. She would tell Martha, "All men are after only one thing, honey, and once they've had it, they'll neglect you until they crave it again."

She was talking about sex, of course. "You are just a dog's dinner to Carl, just like I was to Frank, honey," Mildred would say to young Martha. Martha at first did not believe that Carl was like that, but her mother kept on getting inside her head. All of Martha's friends disagreed with her mother, but Martha ignored them. Mildred would tell her, "Your friends don't know the real Carl, honey. That same Carl who gets you drunk on champagne and then takes advantage of you. That same Carl who plays devious pranks on you for his own sick amusement. He is just like Frank," Mildred would tell Martha. After months of this, Martha, too, started to turn on Carl. He soon started to figure out that it was her mother's influence that was turning her against him.

He did not want to say anything as Mildred was going senile due to what had happened with Frank. As a result, it was a delicate situation for him to approach. One evening, Carl got up in the middle of the night to get a glass of water. When he came back to bed, he tripped and spilt the water on his wife. Martha was incensed. She figured it was another one of Carl's devious pranks. She kicked Carl out of the room, so he slept on the sofa that night. When he awoke, Martha was gone and so were half of her belongings. She had moved out of the house to stay with her mother. She stayed there for a week, but her mother was being very strange. Martha ended up taking care of her mother as she was going even more senile.

One day, when Martha returned from work, she found her mother collapsed on the floor. She had overdosed on her Clozapine tablets which she was taking for her Schizophrenia. Mildred had finally lost the plot and killed herself. Martha called for an ambulance, but it was too late. She was already dead. She phoned Carl to tell him the news. He raced over to the house but when he arrived, Martha told him to go away again.

A few days later, there was a knock at Mildred's door. It was a forensic officer. The forensic explained to Martha that Mildred had been taking her schizophrenia tablets way before Frank had allegedly been beating her. It turned out that Frank had not been beating her mother at all. It was all in Mildred's head. Frank, completely innocent, was immediately released from prison. It turned out that his wife Mildred was self-harming due to her Schizophrenia. Her illness was the result of a miscarriage from her first marriage.

This was the reason her former husband, Roy, left her. Mildred never told Frank or Martha about her Schizophrenia, as she did not want them to abandon her as well. Sadly, Mildred's health had gradually deteriorated due to her addiction to the Clozapine tablets. Frank and Martha had both been unaware of her problem. They found out the truth through Mildred's diary, which she had kept hidden away. She had kept everything concealed from them for all these years, and never spoke of her Schizophrenia to anyone.

Mildred had been using her Schizophrenia tablets for a long time before she had even met Frank. She would wait till Frank was out of the house and then take two every few hours. She started becoming confused as to what was going on in her life. She really believed that Frank was beating her, just the same way she believed Carl was abusing her daughter Martha. After Mildred's funeral, Martha stayed with her father Frank to keep him company until he was comfortable enough to be on his own again. Martha then returned home to Carl who welcomed her with open arms and a romantic meal.

Two weeks later, Carl got down on one knee and proposed to Martha, but Martha said, "No!"

Carl's face dropped as Martha once again went to walk out the door. She then turned around and started laughing at Carl as she yelled, "Gotcha!" She was only kidding.

"I can't believe you did that," said Carl while checking his pulse.

"Ha-ha" laughed Martha, "I was just getting you back for all the pranks you've played on me in the past," she said to Carl as she threw herself into his willing arms. Martha then looked at Carl and said, "Of course I will marry you; you fool."

Carl then smiled back at Martha, then he picked her up and took her upstairs to the bedroom to celebrate their engagement.

Life and its Pages

by Padmini Peteri

"Aadya! Aadya! wake up what is wrong with you?"

"Omg what the hell is wrong with her, why did she faint?" I heard another voice.

There was a lot of chaos in the classroom, classmates, friends crying out my name.

They were shaking me, and I felt numb with grief. I was wondering if anyone could feel both emptiness and pain at the same time, but I did. I could feel my pounding heart, my eyes burning, the urge to puke. I felt breathless like my throat was being crushed.

I heard another voice blurring out, "Go call ma'am. She needs help."

A few hours later, I woke up to the hospital smelling of Dettol, with a glucose syringe on my wrist. My friend Vani was right next to me sobbing her heart out, and Ritika ma'am standing at the corner of the room. My body was overcome with guilt, pain, and my limbs felt heavy to the extent I could not move. My head was throbbing, eyes blurred. I tried to talk but the guilt would not let me.

Ma'am came over to me, touched my head and said, "Your parents are on the way. Are you okay, Aadya? I'm sorry that I did not notice how hurt you were."

I wanted to express the torment I was in, but could not say a word, and cried like a baby in her arms.

"It is alright, Aadya, cry as much as you want. I am right here," whispered ma'am. Those words were so comforting that I cried myself to sleep.

I woke up a few hours later with a headache and saw my dad sitting next to my bed and mom at the other end of the room. They were so quiet that I could feel the ticking sound of the clock.

"Hi, Dad," I murmured.

Dad just stared at me with disappointment and said, "How are you feeling?"

"Why did you have to take an overdose of medicines? You're only 17. Why the hell would you take such an extreme step? Why did you attempt suicide?" Maa screamed.

Her words pierced my heart and I wanted to run away from them like I always felt.

Dad scorned her and said, "Will you please stay quiet?"

"Yes, you always want me to keep quiet; it is like I am the culprit, pushing your daughter into this mess." And she barged out of the room as angry as she could be.

Dad kissed my forehead and said, "Why don't you take a break from college? You can come home and spend some time with me or your mom, and you will feel better." I just wanted to say no, but something in me craved for a place to crash on, to cry forever undisturbed by college.

My dad left to call the nurse, and my memories were back to the days when my parents were happy and together. The moment they divorced; my life was twisted. It felt aimless like I was going in a direction that would only lead to hell. I could not choose to live with one parent, so I shifted to Hyderabad for my graduation and started living in a hostel, and things turned pathetic each passing day. It made me feel guilty about everything and nothing. To me life is a burden.

After spending a few days with dad, I went back to college feeling as bad as I could. He tried to talk about how I feel, but all I did was just lie on the bed watching the ceiling. Nevertheless, I promised him that I would not hurt myself, but I doubt if my thoughts could stay calm.

My classmates were polite enough not to talk about my failed attempt, instead they welcomed me with a warm hug, yet I wanted to run away.

It was English class and Ritika ma'am came smiling as she always did.

She said, "Today, let us not have an English class, let us have a life skills class. I should have taken this class long ago but it's never too late for the right students."

"Yes ma'am!" We all shouted like excited toddlers in kindergarten.

"So, does anyone want to speak about the worst days of their life? Anyone?"

"It was when I flunked in accounts exam," Riya muttered.

"When my boyfriend cheated on me, ma'am," sighed Priya.

"When my dog died, ma'am," said Manju.

Priya diverted saying, "I am sure you have no worries, ma'am, because you are always smiling."

Ma'am scorned and said, "Since I smile all the time, you think I am happy? Since it is my turn, I will talk about the worst part of my life."

"This story is about a 20-year-old me. The time when I looked into the mirror and could not find myself. I saw a mysterious, heartbroken, regretful, guilty, low, exhausted person whose eyes were captured by sadness, and voice taken over by an echo. I felt so worn out that my every breath seemed like a thousand needles were being pricked into my body and soul. It felt like the demons took over my soul and were trying to break it into pieces. My heart was filled with rage, sadness, guilt, and hopelessness. I was more irritated that I had no reason to feel the way I felt.

"I haven't slept for months. And even if I did sleep, that would only last for a few minutes, and I would wake up to an unreasonable feeling that haunts and pierces me every second of my existence, like something in my head was telling me to die or to hurt myself to vanish the pain."

The whole class stared at Ma'am as she took a deep breath and sipped some water. I felt connected to the story because the way I feel was what she is describing. I thought no one could feel the pain I am going through but ma'am experienced it and I felt a ray of hope for myself.

Ma'am continued saying, "Did you know how students felt about food? Food was unbearable to me, it felt like the food was talking to me. telling me to get lost, it sounded like I was not worthy to eat, when so many people out there were starving. It made me feel guilty to look at food for reasons even I did not know, nor I know to this day. I could try and eat when people were around me, but the agony crushed me, and I would not eat for days and still survive on cookies and coffee and act like I was fine. I felt a sense of hopelessness, miserable for weeks.

"This did go on for months, and I did not know the reason why my brain put my soul in hell, why I felt that my body was being ripped into pieces. And the amount of tiredness I felt was unbelievable, and it felt like I was fighting a battle, though all I did all day was just lie on my bed and look at the fan and occasionally cry when family did not observe. I lost interest in all the things I once enjoyed, I no longer wanted to eat or read or do those things I thoroughly loved.

"I would stay home all day on my bed and do nothing, because even getting off my bed seemed like a burden. There were times when I had unhealthy thoughts; thoughts that took over everything that was good in me and turned me into a person I hated. There were voices in my head that were constantly telling me to bang my head against the wall, thoughts, voices that wanted to inflict pain upon me. The demons were torturing me. And there also came a time when I wanted to give it up all and even considered suicide, but I knew I did not want to kill myself. I just wanted to let go of the pain. I know this is bad right now, but back then, I really wanted to inflict pain on myself so much that I was ready to die.

"And there was this one day, a moment I really did something bad to myself that made me realise this is not me." Every soul in the class was quiet; tongue-tied. My tears were not stopping. I could feel the battle ma'am went through because that is what I am going through.

Ma'am wiped off her tears and said, "That was the time when I realised, I needed help. On discussing with my dad and doctor, I was diagnosed with severe depression. It was a battle; every day, I tried not to succumb to the agony, the guilt. It was so terrible that I could give up, but I fought it like a battle, and I won like a warrior. I'm proud of myself for going through tremendous pain and yet survive and become the stronger version of myself. I did not have a reason to feel depressed, everything was beyond perfect, but depression takes over you when you least expect it."

Ma'am looked at me and said, "Depression does two things to you. You either win a battle or lose a battle. What you choose defines you. It defines how you want to be remembered! I'm here to help you all."

When ma'am said those words to me, I could no longer hold my tears or the pain, I ran and hugged her. She whispered to me, "It is time you fight your battle and win it, Aadya!"

I smiled with a huge relief, "I'm ready!"

Yet, Not Found

by Jigyasa Tandon

This story covers a relationship of a young girl with her old friend who is older to her. It is written in the form of an engagement letter which she plans to write to him to confess that she is in conflicted love with him. She had been in denial for some time, claiming that a feeling of emptiness is nothing other than a change of routine and adjustment to a new environment. But now, she is discovering love because of the stage of life she is in.

Also at present, she is working on a project which is centred around exploration of love among humans. She soon realises in due course of separation she was with him that she had been in fatuous love with a drop of addiction in it. Hence, the anxiety was understood as emptiness at war with her ideals and goals. He, over conversations, conveyed that he likes girls to be dressed in a particular way and now she has been continuing his taste for a while. The current workplace excites her due to the amazing group she had become friends with. Or it could be seen as a guy approaching her and she enjoyed that attention, giving in thinking that maybe this is a road of recovery for her.

Dear Sagar,

With a little astonishment and surprise, you must be opening this letter. After all, receiving something from old connections is a situation of rarity. Indeed, this word piece reaching you, too, chose an offbeat derailment after years of denied communication and a sense of unfamiliarity that usually grows between once known people. With the hope that you have been doing fine in your land of contentment, I am writing to you with some courage to voice myself and reply to your unanswered letter received 7 years ago.

While I write this letter, I am sitting behind a caged window, with one of the rods slightly curved. A sign that defines that somewhere someone tried to free himself/herself from the inner bondages and did have a chance to battle the pain and uncomfortable state, s/he would often find herself or himself in. I don't know if you know this state or not, but experiencing it for a while, as my friend mentioned it to me, and she further offered me a piece of advice to see a therapist. She is new to my life scenario; thus, I feel she has this need to push me out of the mental ache she has observed in me based on the steam of conversations and significant patterns of complicated behaviours I involve myself in. I don't offer disagreement to her; I always fall back upon the thought that you introduced me to. You cited not everyone is prepared to fight, but, if you disagree, they feel hurt. This is because they might have formed that thought after a lot of deliberations with oneself in their life. The act of simply communicating a thought is too very complex.

Somehow, what we ideally think about doesn't reflect in the way we put forward the point to others. Here we find ourselves held back due to existing barriers in our own space such that we aren't even aware of them. As a result, the shadow of strong noise hovers over ears leading to a bunch of pieces of advice aimlessly thrown at the listener. This also involves an instant need to deliver a response in the dialogue, as taking charge of the situation is the natural act of a human being. Adopting this fashion, they also reveal a fact that they want to put an end to the exchange of words over the pain of another person, for they have suggested the best. If you continue to drag your problem by not signing up for change, it's simply means you are being lazy and irresponsible.

She further adds, she sees a part of her in me and she doesn't want me to struggle as she did for a long time. At this stance, with a lot of passage of time, she has overcome her problem and feels better about herself. Her partner is one of the prominent reasons for motivating her through the bed of thrones turning to roses. I refrain from judging her, since life has not been fair to anyone. The texture of her life may have had an absence of male comfort and the harsh lines drawn across would have made an impression on her that there definitely exists a prince who would come on a white unicorn. He would resolve her life with all the pinks she had always admired, away from the pinching red that painted most of her life.

Well, I carried back her thought to another mellow night of my routine. Alone is a relief, I put myself in. Away from family, in a small studio apartment, structured by visions of the owner's choice, it's a sight for sore eyes. Despite spending 3 years, I have just been able to give a slight degree of concession of assurance. It has become a distant acquaintance I have become accustomed to with a will of the force. But your recommendation to Amit, that day when he was defeated with the placement he got selected for. A swanky individual in 4th year of college, who used to always give in to the stance of authority and objectivity shown by other individuals, since this was the language, he knew most of his life. At the end of the day, he lost the skill of decision-making for himself. Everyone somewhere knew his fate. But no one chose to speak to him about it, as weaknesses are to be hidden under the blanket. You came across like a hero that day, where you questioned him- "Why do you think you deserved better?" and without the slightest thought, he spurted "because I have always complied to rules and did what was asked to be done! And my grades reflected this too." A smile ran across your face, and you made him sit, and asked him, "And in all of this, where were you?" An experience becoming a lifetime guide, that your development is golden; however, your growth is platinum – a condition which is rare and stable. It shapes you in a way, where you come closer to yourself, appreciating what you encompass, discovering what you are made for, and defining your success. This is away from what we are taught to comply with a threat of possible wrecked life as an alternative.

Today, I might scuffle for a house or city, but it's temporary to consider, my augmentation is something that'll ultimately matter. With this thought, I arranged myself for discourse with my limited and accessible mind. Drawing from Shefali's example, I thought to give Anshuman a chance to come closer to my comprehension of life, a step closer for him to acknowledge pragmatic reflection of existence. Unlike the rumoured stern image that people have of me. To calculate, he is fond of my dressing, he says I carry unconventional attire for how a modern woman is perceived. Do you remember how you used to describe "bindi" and earrings just add flavour to Indian clothing? That's what exactly I carry today – a classic pick. Plain long suits, coloured dupattas, a decent bindi, and long earrings. Moreover, we seem to have common thoughts, interests, and the fact that he holds high regard for Urdu and poetry. I can pretty much deduce that we can be good companions.

Over weeks, months, today, I agree with how Miss had expressed that, once you have dealt with the strain of trauma, you can agree to love in any form because it gives you a feeling of being addressed and heard as a person with soft emotions beyond a tough demeanour you kept dealing with hassles daily. Yes, love is the music I am tuned to these days. Unbelievable? I sometimes recall the debates we had on love, where I was always against the idea of it, as for me a perfect man never exists, and you tried your best to convince me that a sculpture of perfection is acceptance of positives and negatives.

Also, it involves constant active-passive action, otherwise, love becomes a story to share to discourage love as an aspect of life. I fathom my naïve nature was a barrier to understand the intricacies of a simple verb of giving affection to someone.

I am not writing this letter to tell you how fantastic my life has become with a considerable group of friends who speak the dialect of care, compassion, and sensitivity to realize the different emotions a person goes through. They are a blessing in disguise. Unlike, the memories of what felt more like making the best efforts to match the definition of friendship.

To quote the real reason behind this letter is to tell you that I took Shefali's suggestion to seek therapy. Through disorderly numbered 45 minute long-sessions I have taken so far, I come to realise that I was bothered by the question you expected a reply to in the last letter you wrote to me. Where you expressed that your portrayal of care like an elder one is merely a tender friendship, and you cannot fall in love with someone with such varied pursuits as him. You felt that I was merely an attention-seeking doll and came up with problems every day to have a chance to spend time. It reflected more of my incapability to resolve my issues and cowardice to not be able to express my real feelings. You further wrote I am a person tightened by stereotypes, and my actions are always restricted. You feel you are more like a guide to me, who is motivated to learn under the backyard tree on the campus. Solving the situation of the faltered idea of adoration, you demarcated it as a relation of a fragile alliance between you and me.

I want to clear the air that I was never in love with you. Instead, I was a person who found me influenced by the power of your charm. Today, I have found my charm. Yet, I have lost myself in the battle to become mature, as you had made me make the goal of leaving my childlike behaviours behind, one day.

Battle of Hearts

by Jagruthi Kommuri

Do you feel the battle,
In your heart that rages?
Surrounded by ribs
Which works as cages,

Can you ever stop that,
Or put it out in your words?
Do you just wait for it to calm,
As to expound it is hard.

Is the heart bound to be caged?
Cause it wants to be wild and free,
But don't you know the story of it?
It knows no boundaries.

As long as there's beat to the heart,
This battle is never going to stop,
And you'll become a warrior one day,
As you master hiding every tear drop.

The battle of heart isn't about winning,
Sometimes you do lose,
This world messed up the meanings,
And left us with no clues.

There's a battle for every heart,
A memory and a mystery,
When time starts to reveal its part,
Every battle becomes a history.

Choice

by Jagruthi Kommuri

How far will you run?
How long will you hide?
One day or day one,
Is your choice to decide.

As for every dusk there is dawn,
From some things you go to move on,
Hoping on silver lining,
Of all the bad timing.

Good or bad is a choice you make,
For some things that are worth, your heart will ache,
No matter what life has in store for you,
At least to yourself, learn to be true.

But when you got to make a choice,
Make it a good one,
For how long will you hide, my friend?
How far will you run?

All the Love in My Heart

by Anu Nair

I had been practicing for almost 2 hours, and suddenly my mom knocked on the door and said, "Sweetie, you need to get ready and get downstairs in the next 10 minutes or you will be late." I looked at the clock hanging on my wall and realised that Mom was right.

I had to get ready, or else I would miss the bus. I quickly got dressed, kissed my cat goodbye, grabbed my guitar and went downstairs. I picked up a slice of toast from my plate, kissed my mom on the cheek and yelled a quick goodbye. I rushed to the bus stop right in time for the bus. I got in and quickly scanned the seats for my best friend, and she waved at me, "Here, Eva!" and patted the seat next to her. I looked at her in confusion, "What's going on, Mar?" I asked her. Mar's real name was Mariah, but I call her Mar because she is my best friend in the whole school, no, actually... in the whole world!

We've known each other since the past 6 years. In all the years that I have known her, she never looked this happy and giggly, apart from the time when she won the first prize at the dance competition. She smiled at me brightly and said, "One of my oldest best friends just moved here and she is going to be studying at our school!"

"Who, Lily?" I asked her. I knew all her friends before she moved to our town, and I had heard a lot about Lily. "Yes!" She squealed. I was really excited to meet Lily and get to know her. We finally reached school and got down from the bus. As we walked into the school building, we saw a group of boys and girls standing in a corner.

"What's going on today?" Mar asked me. I just shrugged and tried to stand on my toes to get a better look, but obviously, I couldn't see anything. Just as we were about to walk away and get to our classes, we heard someone yell out "Mar!" from the group. We turned around and saw a beautiful girl coming out from the centre of the group. The students made way for her, and it looked as if she was a goddess.

Mar squealed and hugged her, and they both jumped around like excited 10-year-olds. It was at this moment that I got a very good look at her. She looked at least 4 inches taller than me and was really thin with long brown hair that was perfectly curled at the ends. Her clothes also complimented her so well, as if they were made only for her.

Lily and Mar finally finished their girly hugs and squeals and came towards me. Mar introduced us to each other, which wasn't necessary at all since I knew a lot about her, and she knew about me as well. As we were heading to class, I noticed that a lot of people were looking at us, especially Lily. Lily and Mar had the same class, so I waved at them and went to my own class. Throughout all the classes, I couldn't stop thinking about how pretty and gorgeous Lily was. Mar had told me that she was also really good at studies and also regularly played at theatres and drama. She was the perfect girl.

As I sat in English class, I couldn't help but compare myself to her; she wore all the pretty dresses and jewellery and I dressed up in oversized clothes. She had perfect, long, smooth hair, and my hair was always a chaotic mess. She was so good in studies, and I was barely able to pass each class. She was an overall achiever and the only thing that I was remotely good at was music.

By the time recess came, I was really depressed and self-conscious. I went to the cafeteria and waited for Mar at our usual place. 10 minutes later, when there was still no sign of her, I finally saw Mar and Lily coming out with a group of students who were all interested in Lily, and it looked like they all wanted to be her friend.

Mar finally noticed me and signalled me to come to them. Seeing all those people around them made me even more self-conscious and insecure. I just shook my head and pointed at my guitar, indicating that I was going to practice. Mar looked sceptical but nodded her head in acknowledgement. I ran to the washroom and looked at myself in the mirror. A girl with messy hair, baggy clothes and bags under her eyes stared back at me. It was the first time I was paying attention to my looks, and I felt very insecure. For the first time in my life, I thought that I looked fat, that I was not pretty enough.

The entire day went by in a flash; usually, I would stay back after school for my music practice, but today I didn't want to. I just wanted to go home and bury myself under the blanket and never come out. Somehow, I went through the practice, got home and immediately went to my room. My mom tried to get me to eat lunch, but I refused. I had decided I would become thin; there would be no more junk food for me, only salads and fruits juices.

I looked at myself in the mirror, and the longer I looked at myself, the more insecure I felt. I noticed all the acne and pimples I had on my face, I noticed every stretch mark on my body and every bruise and scar. I lay in bed, tired and defeated, and decided to listen to some music. As soon as I opened my phone, I got a notification saying that I had a friend request from Lily. I couldn't help myself. I just had to see her profile. I held my breath and clicked on her profile. I was shocked! She had at least four thousand people following her! I checked to see her followers and almost everyone in school was following her.

I lay in bed that night and made many life choices. I decided that my diet would only contain fruits and salads, and I would work out every day and I would make myself look pretty when I went to school and grow my social media following. And that is what I did every single day for the next 2 weeks. I quit eating all my favourite foods and snacks, I spent all my time after school working out and running, I started spending time with the popular kids in school and learnt makeup and dress-up tips from them. I also started posting more and more on social media and I would take every single comment, whether good or bad, to heart.

At the end of 2 weeks, I looked at myself in the mirror and I couldn't believe who I had become. My eyes looked sunken and deep and had dark circles from lack of sleep because I would be up all night growing my social media. My face had even more pimples and acne from using too much makeup, and my head hurt from trying all sorts of crazy hairstyles. I looked lean and thin and did not feel beautiful at all; in fact, I felt really, really sad.

I suddenly got a notification. I looked at my phone and saw that it was a text from my music teacher, who was asking why I hadn't come to practice in the last 2 weeks. I realized that in the last 2 weeks, when I was trying to be someone I was not, I had forgotten to be the real me and do the things that I actually loved.

I lay in bed and cried for almost two hours. Then, I went to the washroom and washed off my makeup. Suddenly, my phone got another notification. I had the urge to look at it and spend the next few hours growing my social media following, sharing all my edited photographs, following people that I don't even know, trying to impress people that don't matter to me at all, and most importantly, being someone I was not and losing the real me in that process. I opened my phone and deleted all my social media accounts. While I was doing that, I noticed that I had many unopened messages from Lily and Mar whom I had completely ignored for the last 2 weeks all because of my insecurities.

I called both of them and invited them home. I sat them down and told them all that had happened, after that, I broke down crying. Mar and Lily hugged me and accepted my apology. After I gathered myself, Lily said, "I know how you felt, and to be honest, I felt so jealous of you." I couldn't believe her!

She continued, "You have the most beautiful voice in the world. You dressed up however you liked and put your comfort over everything else. You didn't waste your time over things like social media and you always seemed to be in such a happy mood. I was so jealous and wanted to be just like you." She said with her head bowed.

Mar looked at us and said, "You see, this is what the outer impression says, but sometimes reality isn't exactly like that. Instead of feeling jealous and insecure about what others have and what we don't we don't have, we should be grateful for what we have and love ourselves for who we are."

And to this day, I follow Mar's words. Every single morning, I look at myself in the mirror and tell myself all the things that I love about myself. I've stopped changing myself for other people, especially people that don't matter to me, instead I spend that time with important people in my life, like my mom, Mar and Lily. And now I'm doing something that I love and I'm truly passionate about – music.

Through my story, I want to inspire you to love yourself no

matter who you are and what others around you are like. Always remember that you deserve all the love in your heart.

Hollow

by Ammarah Safaa

Everybody has glitches
for some they occur as minute errors
for some they set fire
and burn down every concrete wall,
every path you erased,
every corner you concealed,
it seamlessly lifts off the cover.

You find yourself standing in front of this giant being that you
despise
you can't express how you feel
cause it isn't meant to arise.

Who set these barriers on me?
Who took my right to give up away?
Who did this to me?

Maybe all the answers lie in the story I have been feeding on
where the outcome isn't alike the reality
or where the reality isn't like the outcome.

The choice is mine, to see what I wish,
to believe in what I need to,
to know that it's okay to not behave at times,
because nobody can take that from me.

On the Inside

by Joe King

She looks perfect in all of her pictures
With no added filters or glitches
And she captivates minds with wise scriptures
While her jokes have us laughing in stitches

She's always so happy and cheerful
When cheering up those who are tearful
Encouraging all who are fearful
With motives, and not just an earful

Her words are so wisely expressed
Though never unkind or suppressed
And every day she looks her best
So eloquently and modestly dressed

She is blessed with a fortune of wealth
Which she doesn't just spend on herself
She shares it with those who need help
Like those who are poor with ill health

Her life is not boring, nor stressful
Maybe it's because she's successful
But even so, she is respectful
To those on a far lower level

There is nothing her perfect life lacks
She's married with kids, those are facts
And though she lives life to the max
She still has the time to relax

She's gifted at dancing and singing
So blessed since the very beginning
She's desired, as her phone keeps on ringing
Compared to us losers, she's winning

She's winning without even trying
And no one has seen this girl crying
She says, "I don't cry", but she's lying
As on the inside she is dying.

But – She – Will – Not - Admit - It

As – She – Thinks – The – World - Won't – Get - It

Path to Solace

by Tanishq Malik

Down the hill a sacred path goes.

Which was full of dear friends and cruel foes,

Foes gave challenges and friends gave pain,

The intensity of it was too insane,

As the friends were like bush of rose,

Looking lovely but having cruel nature than the foes,

The bush was full of thorns and pleasant fumes,

But the foes were like hated bitter legumes.

After crossing a half mile down,

The pleasant atmosphere changed into sudden frown,

I couldn't keep up with the pace,

As my soul had lost the race,

My all hopes were shattered,

As my happiness in the bitterness of pain was scattered,

I fell with my broken soul on the rock-hard ground,

My soul almost departed unless I saw helping hands by my surround,

Willing to pick me up and taking me across the obstacles down,

But suddenly sky transformed its colours to golden brown,

I made my mind and they made me rose,
But my heart was shivering with the shivering toes,
It was hard to trust anyone more,
The hands came up I counted four,
They helped me through my pain,
And paved my way through the stormy rain.

Soon a mile was gone,
And all four was with the little fawn,
The path which ought to be thorny was actually a golden one,
Where four beloveds made me as a bright new-born sun,
The bond between five became unbreakable,
That it can lead the path stretched too long,
The all five changed the definition of friendship forever,
As it is impossible to break it by another smart or clever,
The four of them became lifelines of my soul,
And completed my life as a whole.

Now I pray,
To the doors of heaven walkway,
The times hard and happy we all face together,
And our bond more than just friendships to last,
And remain untouched for an eternity.

Changing Perspective

by Valerie Lorraine

I have been through a lot in my life. I kept it private, hidden, pent up. I became an island; all to my own in a raging sea that surrounded my shores. It threatened to swallow those sandy shores that I inhabited.

My mind never stopped going over everything. I found joy in just a few things. But those were taken away from me as well. I had closed my eyes to what was happening around me so I could remain in a place that I hid to allow that happiness I felt to surround me. I was oblivious to the fact that I created that feeling. Once that was taken from me, I had to face reality, damaging, shocking truths. That's when I started to heal. It was a painfully hard road. The tears, the fears, the sobs and the facts. Hard truths that I waded through. It was and is a long journey.

Thankfully, I had my writing. It was a huge victory and a landfill for all that contaminated my mind with such gripping pain and confusion. I got to a point where I loved the tears! Those hard sobs came, and I just let them wash over me. I loved the release. I chose gratitude in those moments. I became so thankful it was coming out. And I had learned that after the hard cry was done, I would feel so much better. Every day was a toss-up. Who knew how I would feel?

At first, I was overwhelmed that it would last forever. But then, I started to accept that it was slowly getting better. Some days were pretty good; others were rough, a real mountainous rollercoaster ride I wanted to get off. I started to understand I would get through this. Each day would pass; what I made of it was up to me. I chose to be gentle with myself and allow it to happen, to just be with it. I think that was the biggest blessing, to accept and be gentle with myself!

And heal I did! Slowly, at my own pace; mostly alone. Solitude was my companion. And I welcomed it. Just me and my thoughts. I did have people I could reach when needed. That was a blessing. I stood in the faith that strength was a renewable resource. One that I could stand with and never use up. It just always was there. Even when I felt my weakest and so bare and withered.

Truth be told, I needed those days. The contrast between weak, tired and mentally impoverished against empowerment, alert and gaining strength had shown me glimmers of light and hope. Here was the opportunity to see something new in myself. I chose in those days, way back then to live in gratitude. And that was a game changer. It gave me life. I really didn't know it then. But I found a little etch. A few things every day that I was grateful for. And I named them. Every night I went to bed and told the Universe what I was proud of myself for. Sometimes, more often than I can count, it was that I was able to close my eyes to another day and let sleep take over.

And slowly, without even realizing what was happening to me, I found a way to perfectly love the imperfect me. It became a deep self-love that bloomed. And love gave space for joy, stability and a firm foundation. The rock I was climbing onto was a pure foundation with a beautiful view. The path there was never clear nor without forks in the road. It was not an easy journey. It was certainly Everest, and I did require an oxygen tank to help me breath, a Sherpa to guide me, and many plateau-basecamps to stop and rest.

My Sherpa was my trust and belief in the Universe, my reverence in that She, The Universe wanted me to succeed and be blessed. I used people. That may sound wrong. But I used them in the best way possible. Trust is so difficult for me, but I did give into it. I found trusted people, and I opened up to my comfort level. I used what they gave me. And that was their time and their ear, their voice. Such a gift. Of course, I barely knew what a gift it was at that time. I just knew I needed it. I included it in my gratitude. That gratitude was never heavy as was the burdens I had carried. But as my gratitude grew, I found I put down the burdens so I could carry more of that beautiful gratitude. And my smile widened every time.

Falling is scary, painful and usually comes with bruises and a bloody mess. There seems to be nothing good about falling. But then, I came to this, for myself. And trust me, the time it took to succumb to this epiphany was cavernous! The best thing about falling is knowing that you can rise again. The wrong people fall off. You learn to accept those people who stay, because everyone comes with flaws, and not everyone can fall off! Family is a great example to those who cannot fall off. And family, ah, don't they just hold all our triggers? But it's my gun so if I don't load it, they can have that trigger finger.

My writing saved me. I hold the most gratitude in that I found it. Or maybe it found me. The words were at times almost spoken to me. So powerfully that I had no choice but to write it. I was flawed. Deeply flawed. But those writings were pure. Pure energy, pure emotion and certainly pure passion! And it came out from me and flowed.

They were intensely private to me. No one read them. Well, one person. I shared it all with just one person. And some things remain a struggle to share. As is this piece. I had to wander away from writing it and sit with how I could really put this out there, for everyone to read. Baring my soul and the worst of me. But really the worst of me? I mean, it's a part of me, the me I love. The worst times in my life and all I lost I had to find gratitude for. I'd rather be this me than have those people and those things.

It still pulls at the heart. But I consider those lessons. Things I will strive to see, and steer clear of getting caught up in again.

When I see how my writing and my experiences affects others, I begin to share more and more intimate works. Even though it shocks my system to let it out, so publicly. But who am I to turn down a write? It's a chance to grow, to learn from what may hit the page. Every experience turns to new leaves budding on the Tree of Self-Knowledge. I found something in putting out my work. A huge connection of people whom I could not do without. And that is the biggest blessing the Universe has given me. Without the falling, the struggles and the weariness, I would not be here. So yes, I find great gratitude in knowing that my pain, and the stars I constantly wished upon surely knew it was a painful place... but it healed me and grew me into something so new and vital. I pray that everyone finds themselves in this way!

The time came for us to part

I'd had enough

You showed me the best, I believed that was truly you

And then it seeped out

Cried to be seen

You couldn't keep it under the veil

I saw

I saw you
And I didn't like the bits and pieces
And finally, you showed me it all
I could no longer ignore my heart
It hurt
That you would turn into this
Right in front of me
Everything I believed you to be
Everything I wanted you to be
Gone
The pain of it all didn't stay for long
I know what I want and it sure isn't you
I'd rather sit alone with my thoughts
I'd rather fill my life with my own joy
Then sit in eternity stuck with you
There is such peace in choosing me
And knowing my worth
My inner beauty sucked you into my world
But it also pushed you out when it was time to go
Each scar on my heart is a map through the journey
I'm not at the end
Thank goodness I'm not at the end
For the sake of this journey
I love to travel
And I will happily mar my heart again
And again
Until I find that beautiful serenity.

Confined

by Ammarah Safaa

Mellow rain fell upon the sea
blurring all lines between you and me,
I walked and talked with chaos and silence side by side
monochrome visions that take me on a ride

I saw the times roll by
even before giving me the chance to say goodbye

So is the time spent focussing on wafer of a rainbow packed in
storms
ones that thrillingly torment my soul
with hopes and fears altogether twinning,
somehow, we all know who is winning.

The Spectator

by Shruthi Nataraj

With a burdened soul and broken mind,

I stand at the edge of time,

Trying to understand, what's mine? That feeling of melancholy,

Twists my soul,

It was hard to explain,

It was digging a hole.

I tried to fight, with all my might,

I screamed, "Get out of my sight." But that didn't seem enough.

The bleeding inner wounds,

Silenced my mind,

I knew it was getting out of control, if it wasn't now, I'd lose my mind.

I wish I knew a way out,

To fight this black hole.

My life was falling to pieces,

No one could rescue my soul.

I tried the normal route,

Distracted my mind,

It did the trick for a few days,
But I realized I was falling back into the pit. It dawned to me,
There was no running away,
The problem was my train of thoughts, that kept me at bay.
I decided to acknowledge,
What my heart was trying to say, it's ok to feel sad,
You're the only human, I say!
I lived one day at a time,
Feeling better every day,
Thus, began my journey,
Of healing and feeling gay.
For life happens, my friend!
It isn't in our control,
Remember, you are not your thoughts, just a mere spectator,
Trying to save your soul.

Let Me Take You on A Journey

by John Solomon Arul

Have you ever asked yourself, why is it that we identify ourselves with our strongest emotion? That strong sense of your neurons rattling the limbic system that makes you feel the way you feel. The most real thing to you at the present moment, that defines how you perceive the world around you.

Feel with me this moment, even as you're reading this, what is that one thing that holds that part of your mind, what are those signals that are being sent your way, hoping that you would pay heed to? Let's take that journey for these few minutes we're together in this shared space of our sense of reality. Even as our thoughts are separated by time and space, allow yourself to tap into the power of your soul; that limitless energy that binds us all together as we speak in the language of the one thing that connects the strings through us, being the spiritual beings that we are.

Even as new things keep filling that same space of your mind, you keep wondering why you still feel the same? No matter who or what enters the scene of your periphery, there is this one thing at the back of your head that has such a stronghold on you. Maybe it's that 'one' experience, one offense, one mistake; that one instance that had such a defining impact in your life, that you've started to identify yourself with it. Even as you've heard enough times by now that 'to define is to limit', it seems to be mere words to you now. It just wouldn't go as deep as that 'one' incident has taken root into the depths of your soul. But let's grab a hold of this feeling together, as we're already treading our way down this road.

First things first, why do they say that we limit ourselves when we choose to define our identity with a momentary set of events? Is it simply because when we keep looking back at that one 'tragic' incident or set of events that so 'unfortunately' happened to us, we start adjusting our lens to focus on that particular thing, and now whatever you see in the world is through that same lens. What do you think happens to your vision?! Would you be able to see things as they are anymore, or will it just remind you of how things were? Again, it's not that we can deny these things that have happened in and through us, but it is the very idea of pushing through in spite it all, holding on to that power of your spirit which had so patiently been guiding and feeding you the courage and strength to look yourself in the mirror each waking day with the hope of the testimony of who you could become through all of this.

Let's trace these steps back, even as you're getting reminded of that 'one' thing that I'm talking about right now. Let this following depiction be a trail for your thoughts to follow and go deeper to reverberate at the frequency of your soul. It would be the greatest irony If I limited this to a specific occurrence, especially after I mentioned what it meant to define something, to whoever reading this right now, let your eyes capture these series of words, and allow your own soul to speak to you. Let it shine a light where you've never allowed anything to enter before, let what was put away in obscurity; the things that you've kept locked away which keep eating its way into your core because you haven't given it any further room to move elsewhere, be brought to your consciousness. Take this journey with me...

We, being the emotionally driven creatures that we are, can get so lost sometimes chasing the things that we feel we require, in order to meet a particular need, but don't seem to realise the cost it comes with at the time, simply because we get so caught up going after that one thing, that our field of vision starts pivoting our entire mindset and bodies towards this imaginary make-believe destination point that we think might fulfil us.

What we don't seem to see at the time, is that what we are actually doing is lighting a spark right from the start of this journey, right when we lift our feet off the ground the very first time to take that initial step to head out for what we think we're going after.

Now, this spark will always seem harmless at first. What is it, after all, it's something as small as a thought or feeling you would think right?! But do we really know where this road is going to lead? Now, I don't need to explain what a spark can do in the middle of the forest, which seems to be exactly the place we've positioned ourselves in right now, the middle of nowhere, a place of absolute uncertainty.

Now this fire is going to catch up to us sooner or later, the repercussions of chasing something so meaningless to our identity of who we really are; to the 'things' we try to be, the stuff we try filling ourselves with to quench the superficial needs of the flesh, which leaves our spirit completed depleted.

What is the thing you're running towards that you can truly never get, simply because it's made real only in your head, or more importantly what is that thing you're running away from? The things we arrange in front of us for the world to see, to hide what is really inside. Diving deeper, what is that thing beneath the thing, beneath the other thing, that brings forth certain behaviour in our life. What is the source of these mere manifestations of what is inside, that we so conveniently hide away from ourselves from time to time?

Alright, here, the process refers to the journey backward, to pick up what was lost along the way, those left out parts of us that were burnt in this fire. Isn't it ironic that we wouldn't mind facing a lifetime of hardship in order to get a moment's gratification, but wouldn't want to feel all that same pain intensified in a single moment, to be free from those chains that robbed us of what we once had?

The only way to do that is to go through the pain, to get past those shackles which once seemed to control us, to wobble through the struggle which has clearly been the only reason which was holding us back all along. To truly know that even that feeling of discomfort of pushing through would eventually pass, but what would never pass is the fact that we still remain ignorant to face our past self, to become this more mature and grounded person you could become. Just for the fact that you find that old self more familiar and you hold on to this idea of who you once were, that you're blinded by reality.

Would you rather complain and wallow in self-pity for the stuff which has passed, which by the way, were actions of your own doing, and nothing external. It was a decision to let go of those parts of yourself in exchange for those moments of gratification, or can you find it in yourself to accept what has happened and trace back those steps in simultaneous reflection and aspiration of who you once were and who you could become out of all this. To pick up what 'is' left by the fire, which was caused by your hands, those authentic parts of yourself, those precious pieces that made you; you.

Now, it's important to remember that these burnt pieces might not be recognisable anymore, they were once these glowing rays of sunshine that only belonged within your soul, which was so cheaply traded for something so non-existential.

The only way that these parts could become what they once were is that they return to their natural habitat again. Once back in place, it fills that void that we've never been able to explain all along. It grows back with time to fill in those gaps which you were never able to cover up with anything under the sun.

Which emotion is stronger, the fear of going head-to-head with who you once were, or the courage to look past the experience in order to be that greater version of yourself?

We were so caught up chasing those things that we felt we needed so badly, that we ignored everything else our mind, body, and soul was trying to tell us in the process, those signals that showed up in your frame of vision every once a while, that were so obliviously ignored, letting it pass away into nothingness.

However, if we truly want our intuitions to show up, we've got to invite it to show up and make the space to receive it in the ever so filling space of our consciousness, and you would be surprised to see what you become aware of. The more we get in touch with this still voice of our intuition, the better we can distinguish between the voice of our own with our own biases, and how culture could influence and impact the way we think and make decisions. It's that when these thoughts, ideas, and feelings do actually appear, we would be able to distinctively tell the difference between the two.

Of course, it takes a certain degree of commitment to take up this cause of connecting and getting in tune with yourself, welcoming all that information that your mind, body, and spirit have to share with you, even if it means what you learn and intuit makes you uncomfortable sometimes. This intuition of ours isn't meant to connect us to a superficial sense of feeling good all the time, but rather guide us to the fulfilment of our souls and spirit. Just like a good friend, our intuition doesn't just tell us what we want to hear but rather directs us to a more perennial form of fulfilment. That boundless form of joy we attain when we live our life's purpose, which is to keep growing, keep learning, and keep evolving. I guess that's why they say that 'the places of your greatest isolation, bring the greatest revelations.'

Now, these scars are going to remind you of the fire from time to time, you would remember it so distinctively, that sometimes you would even forget what you were chasing in the first place because the scars have become more real to you right now. The scars remind you of what it cost.

The biggest question which arises out of all this is that 'will things ever be the same again?' Well for a matter of fact, nothing in this universe is meant to be the same. Take a look around, what would happen if something remained the exact way it was its entire lifetime?! Could that be considered as purposeful living? Aren't we going against every law of nature by trying to make something stagnant in our lives, which we evidently know by now, could lead only to infection and disease, even if it means that we would desire this 'perfect life' where our past patterns and lifestyles could repeat itself!

Sometimes, these wounds are inflicted as a result of the environment we're in, we were just oblivious leaves in the middle of a wildfire started by, ironically another oblivious soul...Maybe it's something that happened to you that you would never choose to happen, but it happened anyway. What about then?! What about those open wounds that bleed on the people close to you because you never knew how to close them.

By the way, just know that you aren't any less by the things that have happened to you; those things you feel that have scarred your soul. In fact, you are only more! The wisdom and resilience which was forged through the fire of these circumstances can only add to this burning spirit if you allow it. But, yet again it's a choice you make, and it doesn't always have to be immediate to acknowledge this revelation. That's because 'trust takes time', even when it's with ourselves.

That burning fire of our soul has the power to be strong enough to forge new life and meaning into our lives, which surprise, surprise, also includes our past experiences.

That limitless power of what has been entrusted to each and every one of us is limited only by your strongest thought. You've always had the power to change what meaning you derive out of everything that happens in your life.

Whatever it may be...What starts as a thought which causes these uprearing storms to rage in your head, can also be stopped with a thought! It's all in your hands, the power that we desperately seek in times of trouble and calamity, was always within you the entire time, right from when it was the only thing pushing you through the toughest of times, to the times when you couldn't seem to see straight anymore.

Well, the hardest thing to move past aren't those incidents, it's those burns we inflict on ourselves in the midst of this already raging fire, that we can never really let go of. These wounds that we cause on ourselves that we pretty much sooner or later see as identifying marks of who we think we are as a result of these things happening to us, which is literally one of the biggest lies that we can tell ourselves.

The scars are proof of the power inside of you, the fire inside of you has the power to keep burning parts of your soul away if you let it, but at the same time, it could forge a brand-new definition and version of you. What are you choosing to believe?

Fear to Apathy

by Jennifer Brown

It was a hot August night in 1976 when my thinking shifted from fear to apathy in regard to my father. It was a regular summer evening; I was playing with friends and waiting to be called for dinner. There was always a level of anxiety and fear knowing dad was coming home as I never knew what mood he would be in. This night however, changed the course of the rest of my life.

It was challenging growing up in a home with a bipolar father who had paranoid psychosis. It wasn't only me who took the brunt of his sadistic anger and manipulation as I also had a brother three years older than me. Initially, the abuse was stronger towards my brother up until this experience. It was in my early 20s when I asked him why he treated me so badly. His response was, 'I liked seeing the fire in your eyes'. I remember this day clearly as I was initially shocked with his answer. The result of his response triggered the first time I severed ties with him.

This was only temporary, as I soon became a mother and felt guilty for not involving him.

This is a poem I wrote about that August night:

BMX!

I wanted a bike like the boys had, not a girlie banana-seat one.
I worked all summer delivering newspapers,
and even waking up before the sun.

One time a little ankle biter
didn't want me to put the newspaper down,
I really adored dogs until then
but then feared the smaller ones.

I finally earned enough money
for a knock-off BMX bike,
I felt cool as hell while riding
through the trailer park in my friend's sight.

I learned a bunch of cool new tricks,
I could even fly over the speed bumps.
But one evening the fun ended
when I heard a very loud crunch.

I knew right away my bike was destroyed,
I knew exactly what had happened.
My dad chose to run it over,
all my hard work had then descended.

I had run in the house really quick
as I needed a snack and a drink.
I had left my bike in the driveway
I immediately began to freak.

I didn't want to go outside at that moment,
I knew what would be coming next.
I would be in great, big trouble,
he would be ready to wring my neck.

He came in the house with anger,
spewing loudly how awful I was.
He screamed as loud as he could
how 'I' had dented his truck.

You see our driveway was really long,
at least three cars deep.
He could've easily not wrecked it,
but the lesson he taught was quite steep.

Heaven forbid he honk or just park the truck further down.
It was fun for him to do this
as he knew surely, I would frown.

My dad was an awful human,
fully, through and through.
He got off on destroying my happiness,
as that's how his narcissism grew.

My dad was an awful human,
fully, through and through.
He got off on destroying my happiness,
as that's how his narcissism grew.

I was quite a tomboy growing up as I tried to keep up with my older brother and his friends. They all had BMX bikes and I wanted to be able to go ride with them. We were a low-income family, so I needed to earn the money myself. I was only 13-years old and delivering newspapers was my only option for work. I worked incredibly hard doing this for the summer months without missing a single day. I was so incredibly excited and proud of myself for this accomplishment. The devastation I felt when he ran over my brand-new bike was indescribable at the time. All I was able to do was shut down emotionally to not show any weakness or fear. Anger and silence became my only behaviour towards him from that moment on.

My change in behaviour was fuel for my dad as I mentioned he enjoyed my anger as this excited him. My mom on the other hand was not pleased as she is a passive and traditional woman who avoids conflict at almost any cost. She actively tried to get me to be, 'ladylike' as this next poem explains.

Be Ladylike

"Listen, you need to be ladylike!"
I've heard this countless times throughout my life.
What I've been taught this means is to be compliant and quiet,
to never create any strife.

I've never fully understood why I couldn't speak up,

but I did learn times when it wasn't safe to.

I know if I write down all my thoughts,

ladylike or not, I could say, "Screw you!"

I never did become as she wished, as I had lost touch with the passive and shy girl I had been. This eventually led to my mom divorcing my father as she stated she was fearful one of us would kill the other. I can admit that as a teenager, the thought crossed my mind regularly. So, on my 17th birthday, my mom surprised me with a small new home she had purchased for the two of us to move into. To this day at close to 50 years old, this was the best present I ever received.

Now, as a licensed psychotherapist I became schooled to help others manage their mental health while avoiding receiving treatment myself. This sounds hypocritical, I know, but I was not ready to face my past abuse. I have experienced many forms of abuse over my lifetime, resulting in the diagnosis of Complex Post Traumatic Stress Disorder, commonly known as CPTSD and Major Depressive Disorder.

It took many failed romantic relationships, the last one completely destroying me with confusion over what I had done wrong. I had been seeking therapy prior to the end of the last relationship and had to completely recreate my self-esteem as I had been separated from any sense of confidence. It was as I was gaining my confidence back and recognizing the manipulation I had received and being taken advantage of for my finances that I ended the relationship. The result of making this decision was undoubtedly one of the most painful experiences I have had to date.

I now recognize my patterns of finding unhealthy men who

typically have the same traits of my father including narcissism, gaslighting, belittling and using me for what they want which recently had been my finances. It is humiliating to know that I can recognize for others what I am blind to myself.

This next poem is short but expresses how I had trapped myself without recognizing it by thinking I didn't need help from others:

Self-Inflicted Jail

A self-inflicted jail needs no bars,
You've trapped yourself thinking you need a key.
It takes courage to change your perspectives
or you'll remain there, no rent fee.

I now can own my difficulties and weaknesses and embrace my vulnerabilities as that is where strength is fostered. I had a strong sense to be the 'tough guy' and manage life on my own as being vulnerable growing up was a weakness and could prove physically and emotionally dangerous. I unfortunately took this mentality as truth for most of my life at the cost of heartbreak and confusion.

I now can openly say that I need outside help and the support of others to continue to heal from my past and to forgive myself for poor choices I made without proper knowledge to do otherwise. I am also working on forgiving others which is proving more difficult as I now recognize that I have projected my anger and pain from my abusive father onto other people who did not deserve it. I am still teasing those threads out, but I have faith I will feel freer and more confident upon continuing to pursue happiness.

I genuinely believe not only from my profession but from personal experience that attempting to be strong and being unwilling or open to support outside of yourself is a recipe for heartache. While in that mindset, it is almost impossible to show someone who is not ready that accepting help is a strength and not a weakness. Abuse gets to our inner core and creates negative beliefs about ourselves and the world which unfortunately, tends to backfire on us. Until we have the knowledge to do otherwise, we will continue down a negative path, but once we gain that needed knowledge and inspiration, we all have the opportunity and gift to grow and soar in life.

Writing About Writing
by Dhrumil Sanghrajka

A flirty muse,

Who seduces a recluse.

Gives you a searing pain,

And maybe some literary gain.

A broken heart,

becomes a squiggly art

To the blue sapphires,

In the damsel's attire.

Ideas and thoughts,

First a million and then nought

Making you feel

Either overjoyed or making your keel.

They abandon us when we create fuss,

To make blue ink meet the white,

That gives us joys and flights.

Ideas tease us, they please us
They take off.

They tick us off, those who can writes
Can conquer with literary might.
With fiction or candour
It's a damned ceaseless wonder!

The Loneliness

by Dhrumil Sanghrajka

When you feel alone,

Even amidst a mob.

When you can't help,

But let's escape a sob.

When you hate the gap Between your fingers.

A deafening silence,

Is all that lingers.

When you know, you are so lonely.

All you can think is, if only, if only

Besieged you are,

By the sullen emptiness.

Perfectly are you riddled,

by the bullets of loneliness.

Like a blind man,

In a dark abyss.

You search for a light,

For that someone who's amiss.

A helping hand will appear, keep up the faith.

A light will come forth,

You just have to wait.

The day will come,
When you'll crave for the silence.
You'll find peace within yourself,
The smile will return then.

Human

by Nishtha Dutta

"We never really understand a person until we consider things from their point of view, until we climb inside of their skin and walk around in it."
— Harper Lee, To Kill a Mockingbird.

Did you know that there are over two hundred emotions, and that each of us is capable of feeling about six emotions at any given time? That might sound like a lot, but it's even more than the range of flavours in some ice cream!

Regardless of how many emotions you feel on any given day, it's important to remember that they're all valid. Each emotion has its own purpose and meaning and without them, we would be incapable of experiencing anything at all. Yet today, slowly, we are becoming the ones who are growing lonely, increasingly trying to separate ourselves from others. But is this how life has to be? Is this how we want life to be? In all of human emotions, one that dominates every human is love. "But then, why the hate?" you might ask. Let's see if I can explain humans a little better today.

My knowledge of humans is mostly my knowledge of myself – how I behave around others, be it humans or animals, and also how they behave around me, how I react in difficult situations, adversities and crises – the more I analyse the more I am left with self-doubt and self-judged, which always leaves me in a pool of curiosity and questions. If I am constantly changing, how can I then ever be right to judge others or even question others' actions?

Now that I sit back and check through, are we ever our true selves, or just the illusion we mime living every day that we think we are? Yet just a minute ago, I told you I would try to decipher humans for you. Over the years, I have come to realise that a lot is stirred by how humans think and feel. How I think and feel in any situation always provokes certain types of outcomes, actions and reactions from me.

Let me give you an example here: A while ago, I asked my younger sibling to lend me one of her ink pens. I am fond of fountain ink pens. She said she had to fill ink in it and then give it to me. A few days later, when I reminded her, she said she had to clean them and then give them to me. I asked again two days later, and finally, when I demanded the pens from her, she got furious. But when I found the pens, they were in poor condition, uncleaned, and never taken care of. But rather than telling me the truth and accepting her carelessness, she chose to defend herself. Now, you see, this is basic human nature. Not just her; if I were in a similar spot, I would act the same way. Note: we don't like to be proven wrong about anything. We don't naturally want to be judged. We at all times want to protect ourselves. We always want to protect our image and our hearts.

I find humans an ever-evolving species, not much in terms of appearance maybe, but the way we have evolved with our thinking and thought process. Over the years, I feel humans have, in general, become selfish and heartless. Over the years, we have grown more scared to show our true selves, which could be vulnerable. We have grown so afraid to be crushed and broken or be used that to save our true feelings from an early age, we have learned to lock our heart and emotions to the deepest and darkest pit of ourselves. Thus, over the years, we forget where Davy Jones's chest lies and where we are carrying the keys with ourselves.

But wouldn't it be romantic when one day, one special Calypso finds the keys and then together they look for the chest? But if someone asks me after several little heartbreaks, I will not even wait for my Calypso and would rather be on a march faraway to the land, where like a prized treasure, I can unbox my heart and let nature take care of its beats. My heart finally breathes freedom without the fear of being stabbed out of air again. But even on that lone island, my heart does hear that sweetened litany afar, and me? If you ask me, well, I would by then be long lost in the field of lotos eaters and having those dreams of winning wars and never returning lands' tales.

Yet today, on just a normal rainy Sunday, sitting in my balcony waiting for my mother to bring me tea, I slowly observe the trees swaying in the wind and raindrops trying to glisten the leaves and droplets like tiny crystals of pure heaven finding their humble fall to the soil. I can't help but wonder about humans.

How do we always get to know what kind of a person someone is? The wise will say it's always by observing them; not just by observing them in their good, but more importantly, by how they behave when something they dislike happens. "It's always when a man is in stress that he brings out his true behaviour or nature." Have you ever wondered how an examiner gets to know who is trying to cheat? Simple; they observe, and our actions are what give us away.

Yet, at times, you will notice that we have failed to know a person. That they are not the person we thought them to be. So, should we not trust our own kind? No, even after choosing to go to the land far away, I know the heart does always crave love, warmth and good company. I must say, choose wisely, but then there will always be people who will just get into your inner circle, into your heart just right in. Some people are like that.

In our journey of life, we will meet men and women of every kind, shape and size. Take this as an experience, and experiences can be good or bad. In that case, keep the good ones close and the rest would be your experience for a lifetime. But like I said, may there be that special Calypso and may you, too, find the chest of Davy Jones which holds the heart. Life would not be worth spending if it is not spent with someone dear, may it be a partner, friend or family. In today's busy, fast-paced world, may you find that anchor, that harbour to dock you ship at times. The ocean will always be testy and those will be the times of trials. But no matter how deep the waves, may they never make you forget the shore that you have decided to call home.

Vindictive

by Ammarah Safaa

Transformation through the eyes of a lover,
pulls the creepy curtains by the cover.

I have slowed my speech
I have sowed what I shall reap
somehow the possibilities drain me weak,

Every moment that I tender,
cherishing the surrender,
undoubtedly through the eyes of a lover,

The puzzles that I ought to solve,
needn't be on what my world revolves,
Is it something to rediscover?
or bent on its ways to recover?

Counting Clouds And Daisy Dreams

by Manasi Narreddy

One day,

I'll lay on my back on a gingham blanket and watch fluffy white clouds float across a blue sky.

I'll sit cross-legged on a woven carpet,

eating a slice of pizza with a glass of deep red wine.

I'll spend a hot summer afternoon looking for pretty mugs with delicate hand-painted flowers in a myriad of colours.

I'll run towards the ocean feeling my feet sink into soft sand and cool water,

and stop with my eyes closed,

Listening to waves lapping the shore, one figure on a beach

Bathed in the golden glow of early morning light.

One day, I'll welcome silence and solitude with open arms and a happy heart,

and smile to myself as the day goes on.

A Journey to Change

by Nishtha Dutta

S itting in the chai shop outside the corporate building of Cyber City Corporate Hub Gurgaon, I'm watching people running past each other to get to the same seat, the same office that they get to every day. I know my phone will ring any minute now, and my office colleague a.k.a best friend will call me to let me know that the morning briefing is about to begin, and like a lazy ass, I will drag myself up to the seventh floor to the IT department's small cubicle where I have been to every morning without fail, a place where my mind ceases to be. Lunch breaks with the same cafeteria food which makes every soul miss home with vengeance, and the sudden urge to book a ticket back home, to where mom's home cooked Tinda and Kaddu fry is much more delicious than everything here.

I answer the cell vibrating in my pants pocket. "Hi."

"Varun! Where have you been? Are you still having that stupid thadi wali chai? Bro, get your ass up here. Boss is about to get to the meeting room." And with that, I am up to my corporate office to slog like a corporate ass. "What's up, bro?"

But no, Shatish looks at me with mock anger and says, "Why do you have to be late for this meeting, and why is that tea more important than briefing for you? And why was your leave was approved, man?"

Laughing, I reply, "Because I applied for it like 2 months before; now, let's go in and let's get it over with!" With that, we both pick our notepads and pens and walk to the meeting room, post which I don't remember anything out of ordinary. I am assigned work for the day, and because I am leaving for a week, I have to make sure everything from my end is finished and Satish has a complete rundown of the same while I will be gone.

Post lunch, I get a call from Ma, telling me to pack all my stuff so that she can wash it, as if I have no idea that every time I travel home, she insists the same. Then, I leave the office, rush to the apartment building I stay in Gurgaon, grab all my luggage, hail an Uber and leave to catch my train to Dehradun.

Hopping on the train and getting all my luggage chained in, I settle to play some games on my phone. I look around, but there is not a single cute girl to chat with, or a proper dude as well, all uncles and aunties. Damn it! It's going to be a long ride home, filled with midnight sleeplessness and loud snores. An absolutely fantastic start to the journey, Varun! I think to myself.

Reaching the Dehradun station by the afternoon next day, I get in the cab for another 45 minutes of driving to get home, but home never comes. When I regain consciousness, my mother is sitting next to me, crying, and I hear a distant noise of my father's angry voice. "What do you mean, 'He won't be able to see, ever'? How dare you! This is a useless hospital, no good. I will take him to a bigger hospital in Delhi, he will be fine…. He will be fine." With that, his voice cracks at the end.

This happened 3 years ago. Today, however, is another one of those journeys that I have started making from Dehradun to Mumbai to consult with an ENT specialist hospital here to get my eyes checked.

"Haan, Ma, yes, yes I got everything. Don't panic, Ma! I will be just fine. Yes, I will call you once I get onboard the train… Of course, you know I would have gotten a flight had I gotten the leave approved a day early, now my only option is a train...should I cancel that? Yes, I will call you later. Bye!" Disconnecting the call with my mother I vent out my frustration on the stupid coffee machine.

Yes, I hate trains and I tried to get a flight. Will mom never let me be. I am a twenty-five-year-old individual now, responsible, and always doing the right thing. I take my bags and punch out by 5 p.m. and then take a taxi to the railway station. After getting settled, I heave a sigh of relief.

*****

At the last minute, her office colleague had been able to get her the lower berth; at least, she can have the window to herself. Soon, she sees the train starting to move, and a young, tall guy comes and sits in front of her. She notices this guy while talking to her mother, and just like every train journey where people talk to each other out of boredom, soon, she starts talking to the guy. Initially, she confirms if the seat is his or the luggage is his, and then proceeds with the introduction "Hi! I am Mitali Ghosh," she says, and gets to know that he is Varun Sinha.

He asks her about her job, and she enquires about his, to which he says that nowadays he works for a local radio station in Dun, and earlier, he worked for an IT corporate firm in Gurgaon. They realise that both of them at one point once worked in the same office compound. Varun is into music and travel. He is headed to Mumbai for a medical appointment. Saying this much, he asks Mita her reason to visit Dehradun, and just like that, a day and half go by in talking.

Varun often asks her to look out the window from time to time and tell him about the view or the water stream flowing by the rain tracks or the mountain and how the view is, and she tells him that it is mesmerising. "See, not so bad, right? You can't say that you hate trains now, or else how will you be able to have such a stunning view from a flight? It's clouds mostly, you know." Varun laughs at this and has to finally agree that travelling via train has its perks, too.

They talk a great deal, and it's always Varun being the optimistic one and Mita being the hyper one. But somehow, both of them feel nice to talk to someone and to get to know a new person. Mita advocates how hard as a person she has to work every day to prove her worth to the world, that every person has to struggle, and struggle doesn't end, explaining to Varun that life has offered him everything easy and that being a middle-class girl, she has to see a lot of hard times for her to get her degree or her job now in a different city and to live alone.

It is while getting off the train at the Dun station that she sees Varun unfolding his walking stick and an old man guiding him off the stairs. Shocked, Mita, while saying goodbye, tries to tell him what she meant in the train while telling him about life being easy, but a smiling Varun cuts her off and says, "Chill, it's quite alright, life has indeed not given anything to me on a silver platter, but it's still okay." Feeling guilty, she asks him to stay in touch, and the old man who guides him off the train is his father. Introducing himself, he says, "Why don't you and your family come and have lunch with us tomorrow if you are free? Varun's mother will love to meet you, and it would be nice."

She said, "No, no, Uncle, how can I impose on you like that?" but on being insisted by Varun and Uncle, she says yes.

Taking a cab to her hotel to meet with the rest of her family, she keeps thinking that she couldn't guess that Varun is blind. She feels bad about the way she kept on harping that life is easy for a boy or for the rich. Seeing her mom and dad at the entrance, she gets emotional. Her little brother Sumit takes her luggage and gives her a half-hug, saying, "You have to share the room with

Mom, and I am stuck with Dad." Later, she tells them about Varun and the lunch invitation to their house the next day.

As decided, post their sight-seeing a little bit in the market, they go to Varun's house which is a big English-style bungalow, not very far away from the main market area a little uphill. Ringing the doorbell, they are welcomed by a middle-aged lady who introduces herself as Mrs. Sinha. Walking in the house which is spacious with a decent lobby space moving further, there is the drawing room to the left and dining room to the right, along with a staircase leading to bedrooms on the first floor. Soon, Mr. Sinha walks to the drawing area to welcome them all, along with Varun. They enjoy a very filling lunch, chicken masala style and lamb biryani, Indian flat bread, cucumber raita and Gulab jamun.

Sitting together for chai, Mrs. Sinha says Varun loves to have masala chai. It's his favourite. Mita finds Varun's family very comfortable to discuss Varun's condition with, and they soon get to know what had happened. Thanking them for the lunch and their lovely hospitality, Mita along with her family, say their goodbyes to the Sinha's and go back to the hotel.

Smiling to herself, Mita looks up from her book that she has been reading and looks at Varun and her brother talking while coming back from the tea stall with hot steaming paper cups of Varun's favourite thadi waali chai. They are back in Dehradun, and right now, sitting in one of the parks along a tea stall. That journey three years ago and her accidental conversation with a stranger on a train from Mumbai to Dehradun changed her life. She will always remember how he looked and how he talked. Not much has changed, but the operation for which Varun and his family had been visiting Mumbai has worked somewhat.

Even though he still can't see very well, now he can at least have some kind of light. They are all now waiting for a donor who will give Varun a pair of eyes. Mita knows that will happen, too, because Varun says it will happen. She has never met a person so positive and affirmative in any situation. He is always hands-on-the-deck never backs down from anything, and always stands strong despite the situation and wears a smile.

Looking at him now, she remembers when once, she asked him why he always walks without his walking stick, and almost every time his doctor advises, he refuses to put on dark sunglasses. He had told her, "People's disability does not cripple them, Mita; it's their acceptance and giving up hope which does. I don't like to wear dark glasses because people always take pity on me in them, but my vision impairment has never stopped me from doing what I wanted to do. Not then, not now, not ever. Yes, I had to adjust my lifestyle a bit, but I still love to do a lot of stuff which I liked to do when I could see."

Over the past years her family had travelled to Dehradun couple of times and Varun's family had come to visit them in Kolkata, too; he absolutely loved Mishti Doi and Durga Puja. She had never thought that she would find a dear friend, a well-wisher on a train. But she absolutely will remain thankful for all flights to have been either booked or out of her budget that day.

"Hey! Miss Lost, are you still with us?" Varun asks.

"Yeah, yeah! Totally. Did you guys get me the packet of biscuits I asked?" and with that, they start chatting like always.

Later, while Sumit is on the phone and Mita is reading her book, Varun is sitting with his earphones on with Mohamad Rafi music slowly singing in his ears, he goes back when he thought that life may be difficult, but he had still managed to find some friends. He hopes to see the world again with all the colours and people and roads and everything. But who would have thought that on one of those stupid train journeys back home from Mumbai, he would find that one person who would become his friend and would appreciate him for what he is and not be just sympathetic to his condition like other people?

Mita is not like other people; she is a different young girl filled with lots of energy. An opinionated one who will always have some observation to make of the world or people around her, but always good at heart. Closing his eyes listening to Rafi, he finds sleep with the winds rustling the leaves on the tree nearby. He thinks to himself, "A lot may be lost but not everything, there is life yet to live."

MEET THE CO-AUTHORS

Achyut Vaidya

He is a professional content marketer, and an aspiring author. He is an introverted daydreamer who usually fails to articulate his thoughts through spoken words and does it (probably) better through written words. Time will tell, so will his efforts, what the future holds for him. You can read his writings on Instagram @wordsthatstir.

Ammarah Safaa

Ammarah has been writing poetry since the past 4 years and was recently published as well; she wishes to grow more in this field and be able to use her voice to reach many more people!

Anu Nair

Anu is a high school student with a love for travelling and creating new worlds through her words. Born and brought up all over the country, she quickly fell in love with travelling to new places and writing about them. Apart from reading and writing, Anu spends many hours listening to music and daydreaming about fantasy worlds. Food and pets are also some of the things that excite her. Being a full-time student and a part-time writer, she is now fulfilling her dream of bringing her stories come to life. She currently lives in the Northernmost part of the country with her family and spends her days studying and writing.

Ankur Mondal

An Ad-filmmaker with over a decade of experience, Ankur has co-authored three books and is a strong advocate of the LGBTQ+ community. When he is not producing commercials, he travels along with his partner to untapped destinations to explore humanity and diversity. He captures the beauty of nature through his video travelogue. Photography, Singing, and writing help him express his unspoken ideas and also connect to his soul and find him his Nirvana.

Deepanshu Joshi

Deepanshu is a Delhi-based writer/ poet who is forever lost in his infinite void, filled with his love for flora and fauna. He likes to spend time sitting in open areas, watching life around him, and learning a new thing each day. A low-key fitness enthusiast, he tries to maintain his sanity by working out. He always carries a pen with him as he believes it's a writer's ornament.

Ayush Panda

Ayush Panda is a student of Psychology at Assam Don Bosco University, India. He acquired a taste for poetry back in high school and wants to write at least one adventure fiction novel. Born in Odisha and raised in Hyderabad, he loves to cook, travel, meet new  people, and finds joy in experiencing new things. The poems he writes stem from his musings and generally revolve around emotions and society. They carry a profuse number of raw emotions and are relatable. He geeks on Greek mythology, horror stories, adventure fiction, and loves watching anime.

Dhrumil Sanghrajka

 Businessman, Bibliophile and Zythophile. At first sight, you'd think that Dhrumil was born with a phone stuck to his ear. Whenever he's not fielding a 100 business calls a day, he lets his mind wander the fertile plains of his imagination. An agnostic who firmly believes in 'Carpe Diem!'

Manasi Narreddy

Manasi Narreddy is a medical student and occasional author, inspired by the depths of human imagination and the power of perspective, and is driven by the passion to share stories navigating mental health with the world. When she's not in class, she can be found with her nose in a book and music blasting away, usually in the company of a mug of coffee.

Harita Odedra

Harita Odedra discovered her love for words when she was twelve. She is passionate about literature and spends her time devouring books. She is also obsessed with dark academia, Greek mythology and binge-watching TV shows. She aspires to become a writer and is currently pursuing her degree in English literature. She loves expressing herself through words, may it be poems, stories or her own blog, @thelitpicture.

Shreya Bhangare

Shreya Bhangare, 26-year-old, is a banker by profession but a vagabond spirit by heart. Growing up with words of Sylvia Plath and Lord Byron, she wishes to be as infinite as the air, to feel as many cultures as possible and to travel the world and maybe one day to the space and beyond. Being a storyteller, she aspires to publish her own novel one day. Everybody around us has a story to tell. And that's where she draws her inspiration from. She is an avid reader who would always be seen with a book in her arms. She loves to share snippets of her heart on her blog called The Unknown Voyager.

You can connect with her on Instagram: @sharayah.poetry, @sharayah.reads.books, on Facebook @Sharayah and Twitter @shreya.bhangare.

Harshitha GR

Harshitha GR is a poet, short-story writer, blogger, an avid reader, and a nature lover. Her immense love for reading made her take the first step to her writing journey by starting her own blog which goes by the name PhenomenalReads. She graduated from Christ (Deemed to be University) with a degree in Business Administration and is now working towards pursuing her dream of writing her own bestselling novel.

Valerie Lorraine

Valerie Lorraine is a free verse poet, speaking on all matters of the heart, turmoil, fears, giving up, letting go and starting again. Her first book Falling is out due March 2022 and her second book will be expected out in Spring 2022. Valerie has been overwhelmed by the responses to her works. Connecting to other artists through poetry is her absolute passion! Through meeting artists of all modalities and seeing them create valuable connections within her community, Valerie has described herself as blessed. She has made Instagram her premier platform to share her work. On Instagram, she hosts many pages as well as her own for open mics and poetry readings.

Find Valerie on: Facebook at Valerie Lorraine Poetic Author; and on Instagram @valerielorraine_poeticauthor.

Joe King

Joe King is a rhyming poet and storyteller who lives in Bourne-mouth, a seaside town on the south coast of England. He likes nothing more than to pick up a pen and inspire others with his words. Writing is a way for Joe to express his emotions and exercise his creative mind in the form of rhyming poetry and storytelling. Joe has a new book (Dark Night of My Soul) which is due for release in a few months' time.

Rafiya Tasneem

Rafiya Tasneem was born in the state of Odisha, although she moved a lot and changed many schools. The one thing which remained constant was her love for writing. One can describe her as a good example of the word multi-talented; she is good at sports, she can sing, she has also attended martial arts, she is good in academics with a love for physics. Apart from all this, she may over love sometimes, but she could never hurt a soul intentionally; she feels the pain of others and tries to express it through her writings and wishes to create a difference in the society through her writings, she believes in the power of literature.

Jagruthi Kommuri

K. Jagruthi an E-commerce graduate, and an MBA student, started writing to express her feelings and loves to write to ignite a little hope and faith in the reader. She's a simple girl who finds solace in words and writes to spread love & positivity to the world. She believes kindness goes a long way when communicated through heart.

Jennifer Brown

Jennifer Brown, LLC, LCSW, is the owner of a private practice psychotherapy clinic in Utah, USA. She runs a community group called Community of Helping Hands that focuses on creative ways to serve her local community and build friendships. She is an author of a children's book and is in the process of a new children's book and compiling her own poetry to be published.

She can be contacted at jenjay1160@gmail.com, #poetryhealingpain #communityofhelpinghands99.

Uma Bokil

A literature graduate who always wanted to work with books, Uma likes to read, write, and explore new genres of life. Her interests vary from food to nature to animals to what-not. (The list keeps on growing.) She currently serves as the Publishing

Manager at Inkfeathers and thoroughly enjoys connecting with writers all around the world. You can find her enjoying the luxury of doing absolutely nothing on Sundays and getting cosy with a new book every now and then.

John Solomon Arul

John Solomon Arul, twenty-two, pursuing architecture with an ever-growing fascination of expression in all of its forms, deeply believes that at the core of each and every creation, is a story waiting to unfold, that flows seamlessly through the streams of circumstance, only to find its way into an ocean of purpose for the world to taste and cherish in its perfect time.

Kashish Lewis

Currently in Bangalore, Kashish Lewis is a poet, author and designer. You will find her at a local bookstore, open mics, cafes or simply rummaging through a stack of books on sale. She talks about mental health, modern-day feminism and other social issues on

her social media pages. Her love for meeting people and learning from new connections brings her to the world of events. Find her debut poetry book 'You Me and Love' online and you can also connect with her on Instagram @kashishlewis to read her latest work.

Manya Kaur Khurana

Manya Kaur Khurana hails from Ludhiana, Punjab. She is a true-crime enthusiast and a lover of naps. She prefers late nights and early mornings (just not the middle of the day). She prefers to write dark and deep things. She discovered her passion for writing years after she was shoved on stage to perform in school. When not writing, she can be found staring at the wall.

Nishtha Dutta

Nishtha Dutta was born in Jaipur, also known as the 'pink city' in Rajasthan. She has completed her masters in both English Literature and MBA Human Resources. She believed literature is as equivalent to life lessons. A literature lover, one can always find her buried nose deep in a book. Likes to narrator her own stories, read them out loud to an audience (specifically on Clubhouse). she loves to write short stories depicting the reality and always believes that one should try to give back to the society and leave it better than they found it.

Jigyasa Tandon

Jigyasa is a trained mental health educationist in NIMHANS, Bangalore, a Counselling Psychologist (Sensitive Groups), teacher, and the author of Echoes of a Rebellious Mind, a collection of poetry.

Manoj Akela

Manoj is a simple man struggling his way through life, like his master before him. It's never easy to face your fears, but the key is to be consistent. The author shares his story to motivate people to never look back and keep going forward no matter the hardships you face.

Padmini Peteri

Padmini Peteri is an avid reader who has a passion for writing her heart out. She writes short stories and poetry. To her, writing is healing and a way of expression. Her poetry collection 'Of Venom and Honey' has been published recently and is well appreciated. She believes in smiling and spreading happiness makes the world a better place to live in. Her poetry writing finds wings on her Instagram @minithoughts_pp.

Pratham Kar

Pratham Kar is a student who grew up observing the wrong side of the tracks very closely from his home in Cuttack, Odisha. He loves to give personalities to problems and often tries to have rational conversations with them. He is studying science but yearns to understand and write about human relations. He loves the skill of formula 1 and the frustration of MLB. He is a young writer who is trying to create compelling characters from simplistic storylines.

Uma Ramaswamy

Uma is a passionate content writer who loves to play with words. It helps that she is an avid reader, exercises fluency in the English language to the maximum, and possesses an active imagination. She is a keen observer of people, and their reactions to various circumstances/situations. These observations serve as the foundation for her real-life stories. Apart from writing, Uma is keenly interested in photography, music and dance, dramatics, travelling, and making friends.

Saniya Shah

Saniya is a doctor who loves books more than blades. A bibliophile, aspiring author and a loving cook, she is good at it all. Her Instagram '@thebookwormcritic', wherein she reviews and recommends books, has been receiving great love and support within a year. An introvert  soul who wishes to make her own path away from the mainstream.

Sarthak Khurana

 Beyond the identity of a working professional breathes a person who is on a journey to find himself & where he belongs. He calls himself a fitness enthusiast who loves travelling and can never live without coffee. An ambivert by nature, he seeks solace and warmth with his writing.

Shaymi Shah

Shaymi Shah is a creative content writer by passion. Most of her writing comes from the observations of everyday life. She tends to have an inclination towards seeing the otherwise common things that happen in life with a different perspective. Today, 

through a lot of practice, she has successfully imbibed in herself the skill of weaving stories – stories that one can easily lose themselves in. She has written for 40 anthologies so far and her debut book of poems has also been published.

Shruthi Nataraj

Shruthi Nataraj is a lover of life, words, and anything that spells art. Being a person with varied interests, she finds her source of happiness and solace in writing and different art forms. An avid reader and traveller, she works at an MNC by the day to pay her bills and writes to feed her soul in the night. A co-author of four anthologies and many more to come. Follow her @the.literary.muse.

Sourav Ganguli

Sourav grew up in Kolkata, India and has been a singer, narrator, a competitive cricketer, and footballer. He's also a bit of a snob about fancy whiskey. When he isn't writing codes, he's probably watching edgy black comedy on Netflix or dreaming of a start- up business. You can drop him a mail at souravganguli23@gmail.com.

Susprihaa Chakraborty

Susprihaa Chakraborty is a dreamer who pirouettes in the world of her imaginations through intricately written pieces that are certain to tug at the heart on your sleeve. Being an architecture student, a vocalist, and a passionate writer, she loves to create visualizations conceivable by everyone where she can express and enhance her view of the world.

Tanishk Singh

Tanishk is a freelance content writer and editor hailing from Varanasi. He loves music and playing the guitar. He is currently at Inkfeathers as a co-author of multiple anthologies and a member of the content services team.

Tanishq Malik

Tanishq Malik is a poet, writer, photographer, and a graphic and content enthusiast. Brought up in Delhi, he is initially focusing on bachelor's in business adminis-tration. He wrote his first short poem in the year 2014 and has been writing since then. He writes in both Hindi and English and is an admin of a well-published writing and photography page.

Toshali Patnaik

A post-graduate enthusiast hoping to author a book someday, traversing through the land of law and logic, fearlessly spawning magic through her poetry.

INKFEATHERS PUBLISHING

India's Most Author Friendly Publishing House

Stay updated about the latest books, anthologies, events, exclusive offers, contests, product giveaways and other things that we do to support authors.

 Inkfeathers Publishing

 @InkfeathersPublishing

 @_Inkfeathers

 @Inkfeathers

 Inkfeathers.com

We'd love to connect with you!